A Puzzle
Without a Box

Linda Hullinger

Copyright © 2002 by Linda Hullinger

ISBN 0-7414-1027-3

Published by:

PUBLISHING.COM

519 West Lancaster Avenue
Haverford, PA 19041-1413
Info@buybooksontheweb.com
www.buybooksontheweb.com
Toll-free (877) BUY BOOK
Local Phone (610) 520-2500
Fax (610) 519-0261

Printed in the United States of America

Printed on Recycled Paper

Published March, 2002

To the Teacher
For his spiritual guidance and protection
and
for keeping me focused
while crossing the log.

Contents

Acknowledgments

I would like to thank the people who have directly and indirectly guided and encouraged me along the way: Conrad Adams, Marci Brown, Martha Corson, Lois Crouse, Nina Day, Bill Dear, Bert Fife, Ruth Jones, Nell Meriwether, Mrs. Perrin, Rita and Wayne Pulley, Lori Rushing, Steve Sasser, Kathy Touchet, Sue Turner, and Denny Vitola.

A special thank you goes out to Betty Hullinger for being an understanding mother-n-law, and a dear friend.

A lifetime of thanks goes to my grandmother, Edna Moss, for sharing her own stories, and for always supporting me 100% no matter how weird things became.

I want to thank Mary Jo McCabe for helping me discover and accept my abilities.

I would also like to thank Pat Talbot for always being there with the right words when I needed her.

I want to thank Lisa and Terry Guidroz for giving me the opportunity to learn what I do is healing for others.

A very special thank you goes to Judy Collier for having the courage to trust in my newfound abilities.

I want to thank John Edward for being the warrior so people like me can fulfill their purpose.

My gratitude goes out to all the mothers who have so generously allowed me to share their children's stories. You know who you are, and I thank you and your children for coming into my world.

I want to thank my spiritual helpers who have made this journey what it is: Edgar, William, Kyle, Jason, Tanya, Emily, and Russ.

A heartfelt thank you goes to my husband, Bob, for always understanding my ups and downs during the writing process, and for never letting me give up.

i

Most importantly, I want to thank my children, Michael, Heather, and Rusty for sharing me with the children on the Other Side.

Last, I want to thank my mother and father for continuing to guide me even after they have crossed over.

Foreword

In the fall of 1996, I met Linda Hullinger. We had enrolled in a spirituality class taught by Mary Jo McCabe. I joined the class in hopes of learning more about the spiritual world. My only son, Kyle, had died in an automobile accident in April, and I was searching for answers. The class met once a week for over two and a half years. There were twelve classmates, and my first impression of Linda was how quiet and reserved she was. I learned that she was happily married and had three children, but it wasn't long before I also learned that she herself had a unique gift. She could connect with the spiritual world and those who had died. Linda brought me hope and comfort concerning Kyle's whereabouts, and I was amazed at her accuracy in connecting the two realms.

During the class, Mary Jo often encouraged Linda to use her abilities to help others, but Linda gave me the impression that she was content with being a wife and mother, not wanting her gift to become the focus of her life. Never could I have envisioned then how Linda would become such a powerful spiritual teacher in my life.

I had been blessed that so many other gifted people had entered my life soon after Kyle's death. I was fortunate to have a private reading with Mary Jo just two months after Kyle's death. Three months later, my husband and I sat opposite John Edward. My interaction with these two amazing psychics literally changed my life. They not only proved to me that Kyle still lived, but they also brought a new meaning to my life. I *knew* Kyle was okay and I had to share with others what I had learned.

Soon afterwards, I began writing my book, *Quit Kissing My Ashes: A Mother's Journey Through Grief*, which is the culmination of Kyle's unrelenting determination to comfort those he left behind. When I needed help with putting the finishing touches on my manuscript, Mary Jo suggested that I contact Linda. Linda had been working on Mary Jo's new book at the time and apparently she was pleased with Linda's work. So I asked Linda for help.

As most of you know, communication with the dead is not a common topic at the dinner table. So having Linda work with me put me at ease. I knew she would be open and receptive to the overwhelming and unbelievable happenings Kyle kept bringing into my life. The joy and comfort that Kyle has brought to both Jim and me because of Linda's ability is truly indescribable.

Later, Linda began working with Kyle in her effort to help other parents who had lost children. I was excited, not only because I know how much comfort she can bring to others who are in pain over the loss of a loved one, but just as importantly, I know how much comfort she can bring to our loved ones who have crossed over

Linda's accuracy in connecting with loved ones on the Other Side shows that, though you may be separated from your loved ones, they are always with you. Death is not an end; it is a miraculous beginning. Linda has proved this to me over and over again and will prove it to you in her book, *A Puzzle Without A Box*. I am thrilled that she is sharing her story, and I am thankful and proud to be a part of it.

> Judy Collier, author of
> *Quit Kissing My Ashes*

Introduction

Over the past few years, I have realized that I can learn a great deal more from the dead than from the living. After all, isn't that what education is all about: learning about things through history, about those who have lived and died?

Science books are filled with names of people who have discovered things that are beneficial to the world but have long since died. History books, literature books, and of course, the testaments of the Bible all perform the same function: they leave a message behind for those who are still alive. I want to accomplish the same thing. I want to leave a message for parents who have lost a child.

In November of 1998, a young spirit who calls himself Edgar entered my life. He has scared me, delighted me, made me laugh out loud, and even led me to find antique typewriters, which I collect. But his mission here has not been to entertain me. Instead it has been to teach me how to help children on the Other Side.

Through my use of clairaudience, I want to relay messages of hope and comfort from Edgar and the other children. Along with that I will tell the story of how Edgar got my attention and brought children from the Other Side into my home.

Edgar guided me to use the analogy of putting together a puzzle as the basis for this book. During the writing process, I learned why. I have always felt as if I was living my life looking for the missing pieces, trying to see the whole picture. Two years ago, Edgar finally decided to show me what I had been searching for.

But before I go any further, I feel that I must introduce my family and friends who have played important roles in my quest to unravel the mysteries of the spirit that I call Edgar.

First, is Bob, my husband, who has been supportive from day one. He doesn't always understand the psychic phenomena that inhabits our lifestyle, but still he remains unshaken by the circumstances. And, on occasion, he mockingly hums the memorable tune to *The Twilight Zone*. Bob has taught me that anything in life can be humorous.

Next, comes my oldest son, Michael, who keeps his distance from my abilities, yet has his own foresight and prophetic dreams that keep him connected to the spirit world. I've always felt that he's gained far more knowledge than his twenty-one years could have allowed, and I've wondered if he's an old soul who has come into my life to keep me grounded. If anything, he's taught me how to stay calm and listen.

Third is my only daughter, Heather, who was practically born with a crystal ball in her hand and who has always kept us from harm in remarkable ways. Now that she has reached her teens and her abilities have increased, we have learned to heed her warnings. She has taught me that what I have is a gift, not a curse.

Fourth is my youngest son, Rusty, who jump-started my healing abilities into action when he developed health problems at a very young age. His easy-going attitude considering all that he has been through inspires me daily. He has taught me how to eat right, take care of my health, and be consistent.

I will also mention Lisa Guidroz who welcomed me to her town and always, with the most sincere concern, gathered folks who could benefit from my abilities.

And, of course, the book would not be complete without my naming Judy Collier, who has continuously given me support by encouraging and believing in me.

Last, but not least, is a friend of times past, Dr. Bill Dear. In the beginning of this adventure, he listened to my paranormal stories with a genuine interest and taught me that an open mind can be where you least expect it.

With all of this said, please allow yourself to open your own mind as I put together the pieces of a puzzle that came without a box.

Chapter One

Getting a Glimpse of the Box

As a young girl growing up in Virginia, I had visions of becoming a mystery writer and having a house full of children. Now over thirty years later, my vision is a reality. I write mysteries and occasionally I have a house full of children. However, in my dreams it never occurred to me that they would not be *my* children and that they would be in their spiritual form rather than their physical form. But they are, each with their own personality traits and each with their particular manner of getting my attention.

In March of 2001, they helped me design a business card, much to my dismay. As always, they showed me they have a glimpse of the bigger picture. Yet, even with something as simple as designing a business card, there are no coincidences, only pieces of the puzzle that haven't come into play yet.

I was sitting at my dining table trying to think of an idea that would work with a lighthouse. The card needed to be ready for the next meeting on Friday at which I would be communicating with children on the Other Side and relaying messages back to their parents.

I knew what I wanted the card to look like. I knew what I wanted on it. Yet, putting it all together was not as easy as it seemed. Finally, after about three days, I actually came up with exactly what I wanted, or so I thought. That was until the children on the Other Side decided it wasn't what they wanted.

Weeks before, I had decided to draw a lighthouse to represent the spiritual teacher who has always shown me the way back home when life has led me into unexpected directions. I wanted to include something symbolic of the spirits on the Other Side who had helped me for the past several years to bring comfort to the families I had met along the way. Then one day I was shown to pick a symbol for each helper and have that symbol be something that had washed ashore. It seemed easy. It wasn't.

The actual drawing was easy, but printing the cards was a lesson in faith. One that I had difficulty with for over a week. I had learned to trust the children on many occasions—even when nothing less than a miracle was needed to correct a situation. They often came through for me when my temper grew short and my faith tended to be rocky.

After several weeks of agonizing, I sketched and completed my "perfect card." I should have noticed the symbolism that something was missing when I reached the shop and the parking lot was empty. Instead I just picked up my sketch and went inside, only to find a man sitting at a desk in an empty room.

"The printing shop has moved. It's off Airline Highway now," he said with a smile.

He gave me full directions, and I climbed back into my van and tried to recall them. A few miles down the road, I took several wrong turns, passed the given street and went farther up the block to make a U-turn. I circled around and tried again, but missed it once more. Determined that I was not going to allow fate to prevent my endeavor, I drove slowly, made the correct turn, then made several other wrong turns before ending up on a dead end road. Finally, I spoke to one of the children on the Other Side. "Kyle, if you want me to have these cards made, then show me a sign." I went to the dead end and tried to maneuver my van around so that I could head back out when a low swooping black crow flew by and landed on the ground near an out-of-place wood duck. Those had been some of my signs from Kyle. He was an animal lover and brought animals to me quite often. I learned the less likely the place an animal appeared, the more significant the message. Since a wood duck represents learning how to get through the many waterways of life, I knew spotting one at that particular time was significant. "Okay, Kyle, then I'm going to try this. But I know there is

4

some holdup, or else I wouldn't be making all these wrong turns."

I turned the van around and as I drove up a little bit farther, there was the printing shop sign. I had no idea how I could have missed it before. It was very obvious. The sign was big. I had to have driven right past it. In retrospect, I believe I just needed confirmation from one of the children that having cards made with this design was the right thing to do.

After going inside and showing the young man at the counter what I wanted on the card, I left my sketch with him, filled out the necessary papers and paid him. He assured me the proofs would be ready in a couple of days for me to come by and check. I left with the feeling that maybe I had the right idea after all, but still there was some doubt about the design that I couldn't figure out.

A day later, the printing shop called to tell me the proofs were ready. I was so excited that I couldn't wait to see them. When I went in and the young man handed me the copy, I took it to the sofa and had a seat to make sure every symbol of every helper was correctly displayed.

One of the children's symbols was a spider, but when the card was printed, the spider was only a blur. I sighed. Edgar represented the spider, and he was just as significant a part of my training as the other children. The spider had to be right. I brought the proof up to the young man and pointed out that it was a blur. Because of the detailed drawing and its tiny form, it did not appear correctly when the proof was made. I told the employee that I would sketch it again and return with a new one.

On the way home, I asked, "Why did you let this happen, Edgar? I want you on the card."

Immediately, I was shown an image of several other children who needed to be included. I was also shown that the star I had drawn to symbolize my daughter, Heather, was not correct. Heather has been a wonderful help to me as I have learned the spiritual aspects of my gift. She could always see what I couldn't concerning the children on the

5

Other Side. I chose the star to represent her because she is so bright with ideas and somehow has seemed to lead the newcomers to us.

As I was shown this image, a Doors song came on the van radio. I knew that was Edgar's confirmation that what I had seen was correct and since Edgar has learned over the years that I am not easily convinced, he added one more confirmation. A car cut right in front of me with the license plate that read "ED." I laughed and shook my head. "Okay, Edgar. I get it. I'll take this home and work on it over the weekend."

Saturday morning, while sitting at the dining table trying to redo the sketch, I asked Heather about the star that I had drawn. She hesitated a moment and in her shy and courteous way said, "Well, that's not exactly what I would want. Let me show you the kind of star I like."

She took my pencil and drew a star that was much better. Edgar was right. He knew she wouldn't speak up and hurt my feelings, so he made sure I would have to come back home and redo the card.

After the star was added to the card with Heather's approval, I took a break from drawing, and Heather and I went to the bookstore. On the way there, I mentioned I had wanted to include a symbol for Jason but couldn't think of anything that would apply to him. He has always been somewhat of a quiet soul using indirect communication in most circumstances. Then I remembered his father had commented to me a few weeks before about a butterfly that had appeared way before its season. So I mentally asked Jason if he wanted to be represented as a butterfly, to show that image to Heather. Within minutes, Heather looked at me in the van and said, "What about a butterfly, Mom?"

I raised an eyebrow and looked her way. "Why would you choose that?"

She shrugged. "I don't know. It's the first thing I thought of."

Immediately after our conversation, a motorcycle roared past us. Jason was killed on a motorcycle. Within minutes of that, I turned into the driveway heading toward the bookstore and someone blew the horn. We didn't recognize the person, but the car was parked right in front of Jason's Deli. Heather and I looked at each other and laughed. A butterfly it would be.

By Monday, I had completed the new sketch and decided to drop it off at the printing shop on my way to a group meeting in Thibodaux, Louisiana.

Tuesday evening, a lady called from the printing shop and left a message that the proofs were in. I cringed. I couldn't bring myself to go back there again so soon. I wanted to see them and I knew they needed to be ready by the coming weekend for my next meeting in a small town near Lafayette, but I just couldn't bring myself to check out the proofs that evening.

Wednesday morning, I braced myself for the worst and went back to the printing shop. This time the spider and the butterfly were both blurred. I became extremely frustrated. Not at the employees, but at the situation. I knew it was another sign that I still hadn't gotten it right, but knowing this didn't make it any easier. I picked up the proofs and told the young man I would try once more to get it right. When I climbed into the van, the employee came out to my car. "We can try to scan it and shrink it up right now in a different way if you want."

"No thanks," I said. "I'll just try once more."

He shrugged and smiled.

I couldn't explain to him that the children on the Other Side weren't happy with my work. So I smiled back and waved as I drove off.

I got home and sat down at the dining table and began drawing the lighthouse again, all the while questioning in my head and aloud why Edgar was allowing this to happen. Twice the spider hadn't turned out, so I knew that Edgar was the one controlling the outcome.

"What is it, Edgar? What am I doing wrong here?" I asked aloud.

I was then shown an image of something that had happened earlier in the day. Heather had torn off a sheet from a calendar that I had given her for Christmas. She showed it to me before going to school. The picture was of a little boy with an "E" on his shirt. She said it had reminded her of Edgar.

Then I realized what Edgar was trying to show me. He wanted just an "E" on the card. Not a spider.

I sat there wondering where I could put an "E" that would fit in a seascape picture. I found the perfect place and drew it in. Then I drew the butterfly in a different location on the paper.

About ten minutes later, I was on my way back to the printing shop. Once I reached the shop, the employees smiled at me and took my newest drawing. I made a point of showing them the "E" and said that it must appear on the card.

Ten minutes after I left the shop and was on my way home, the printing shop called me on my cell phone. The young man had already shrunk the sketch down to size and the "E" had disappeared. I was ready to scream!

Instead, I just said, "I'll be right there."

I picked up the sketch, told them that yes, believe it or not, I was still going to try again and I left.

On the way back home, gripping the wheel, gritting my teeth and steaming, I asked, "What is going on here, guys? Now what have I forgotten?" Right then an eighteen-wheeler with the name Knight on it passed by me. I had never seen one of those trucks before, but I knew immediately who was trying to get my attention. Russ. Knight was his middle name. So I sighed. "Okay, Russ? Is that it? Do you want to be on here, also?" The radio then began playing a Smokey Robinson song. Another sign from Russ. Suddenly my frustration turned to silliness as I began laughing at the whole situation.

Fifteen minutes later, before turning into my subdivision, another Knight truck passed me going a different direction. I knew then what my holdup had been.

Once inside the house, I sat at my desk this time and said, "Okay Russ, what do you want on the card?" I waited but no image came to mind. "You have to hurry," I said, "because I'm running out of time today before the printing shop closes and I need these cards by this weekend."

Still no image. So I guessed. "A musical note?" Finally I sparked a reaction from him because I saw an immediate NO! Then I was shown a bottle. Granted, a bottle would be fitting for something that had washed ashore but I didn't want him to be remembered as an alcoholic. Before I could protest, he began talking to me so loudly in my mind that I had to listen. He reminded me that he had been an alcoholic and it was the part of him that made him who he was, enabling him to help other people. I mentally argued with him about this for a few moments but he told me it was a disease that should not be shunned. I needed to accept his choice of symbols. I had accepted everyone else's.

I agreed. "Well, then, show me a picture of a bottle." I could draw it as long as I had something to go by.

"Look three shelves upward to a book about physics," he said.

I looked up and the book, *Physics for Every Kid*, was there. I had bought it years ago when I was trying to understand physics and thought the children's version would be easier for me to comprehend.

I took the book down from the shelf and on the front of the cover were six bottles. Quickly, I added one to the sketch. Then I was out the door once again.

It was late afternoon and I was tired, frustrated over the whole event, and ready to say forget it. When I started the van, the radio came on and the words sang out, "When life gets too tough, roll with it baby!" I shook my head and began laughing. It was another one of Edgar's confirmations: a Steve Winwood song.

I reached the printing shop for the third time that day and handed them the drawing. They asked me to wait while they shrank it down to save further trips. I waited on edge while they did so. Finally, the young man handed me the paper. I stared at it, ready to cry—but this time with tears of joy! Everything had turned out perfectly! I signed the release form and walked out smiling.

I climbed into my van and asked Edgar, "Happy now?" I started the van and a Doors song was playing. It was done. I finally had their approval.

On the drive back home, I thought about the reasons I had chosen those symbols in the first place. But then it came to me. I didn't choose them. The children on the Other Side did. Each symbol represented an aspect of each person's personality and was a piece of the puzzle given to me to help me learn to trust the bigger picture—my life. Why did Edgar choose spiders and the Doors music to get my attention? Why would Jason choose a butterfly? Why would Kyle bring creatures of nature into view? Why did Russ find it important to teach me about addictions that needed to be healed on the Other Side?

Each child has come to me one by one to teach me about communication from the Other Side. Each spirit has chosen a symbol that has given me another piece to the puzzle. It has taken two full years to see the completed picture. The first piece began with Edgar . . .

Chapter Two

The Pieces Are Scattered

When Edgar first came into my home on that chilly November night, he was in spirit. Of course, we weren't aware of who he was at the time. We just knew that someone was "visiting."

It was about 9:30 that evening, and I was standing in the kitchen stirring my first pot of split pea soup. Over the past few months, I'd had an unusual craving for this soup even though I had never tasted it before in my life.

Once it began cooking, I decided I loved the aroma of fresh celery and thyme, especially, floating throughout the house. As I stirred the soup, I got the feeling that someone was standing to my right, near the oven door, watching me. From the corner of my eye, I could see desert boots, wrinkled jeans and the bottom of a plaid shirt. I jerked my head quickly to the right to see who it was, but the vision vanished. At first, I thought it was my oldest son, Michael. Though he had been in the kitchen earlier wearing a tee shirt and Adidas shorts, I thought for a moment that he might have changed to go out. I stopped stirring the soup and made my way around the corner. I looked into the living room to see if he were walking down the hall, wondering why he didn't speak when he was in the kitchen.

The living room was dark and empty. I walked part way and paused. The soft ticking of the pendulum clock above the fireplace seemed to grow louder. I looked around the room but saw nothing.

I thought for a moment that maybe I'd just imagined it. Then I went down the hall to Michael's room and tapped on his door. He opened it, wearing his white tee shirt and shorts.

"What?" He smiled, his blue eyes twinkling. "What?"

I just shook my head and said, "Nothing. Never mind."

Michael raised his eyebrows, his smile vanishing. "Okay," he said stretching out the syllables, and closed the door.

I walked back into the kitchen, looked down into my pot of boiling, thick, green soup and began stirring again. I kept staring at it and at the same time trying to capture the same vision from the corner of my eye, but I couldn't see anything. Could it have been several strands of my hair hanging down giving the impression that it was someone? No. I knew I had seen desert boots and wrinkled jeans.

Someone is here, I thought. I know it.

The rest of the night I looked over my shoulder, in every corner and cranny I thought a spirit might hang out. I saw nothing. Still, that creepy feeling as if I were being watched followed me everywhere I went.

About ten o'clock that night, my husband, Bob, called from work. He was working what the guys at the chemical plant call a "dog-weekend," from sundown to sunup for three nights in a row.

"What's going on?" he asked.

"I have the feeling that someone's in here," I answered.

There was a long pause and finally he spoke. "You mean like . . .a ghost or something?"

I laughed at his hesitation and then answered, "Yes. Like a ghost or something. It's a guy, I think."

"Oh great. Just what we need," he joked.

"Well, this one is giving me the creeps. I don't have a good feeling about him."

"Tell him to leave."

"Yeah, right," I said. "Let's see what he wants first."

Bob sighed. "So, what else is new?"

"The usual. Heather and Rusty are in their bedrooms watching TV and Michael is working on his computer."

"Well, I can't talk long tonight, because it's been crazy around here."

"Tell me about it."

He laughed.

We talked a bit longer, and hung up.

14

The rest of the night, I continued looking over my shoulder. I even slept with the television on, which I never do. I had a strange feeling something was going on. We had various occurrences over the years, but this was different. There was someone in our house, and I felt that he had no desire to leave anytime soon.

The following night, about 9:15, I made myself comfortable on the sofa in the living room and tried to make mental notes of what I needed to do the next day. A small lamp was burning and the television was off. Heather and Rusty were in the bedroom playing a Nintendo game and Michael had gone into the kitchen to fix himself a bowl of cereal.

As I closed my eyes, the vision of the guy I had seen in the kitchen the night before flashed into my mind again. I strained to think about it, to capture the full visual picture. It vanished again. I wondered why it was still bothering me and why it seemed so important to remember. I had seen apparitions since I was a child, yet this one stayed with me. It was as if I were a part of him, as if I should know him. Though I never got to see his face, I just knew it was a male.

I could hear Michael crunching cereal in the dining room. I knew he thought something was up the night before. I still hadn't told him what I'd seen.

Michael has never had much interest in the spirit world. He would usually dismiss whatever I said on the topic with an "uh huh" look, shake his head, and then walk away. So I knew I'd get the same reaction if I were to tell him about this.

After Michael finished his cereal, he put his empty bowl in the sink and walked into the living room. When he saw me on the sofa, he was startled.

"What?" I asked.

I could tell by the look on his face that he wasn't pretending.

Michael stared at me for a long moment, then ran his hand through his neatly trimmed red hair. "I *know* I just saw you walking down the hall."

I smiled and said, "No. I've been here for about fifteen minutes."

"No, really, Mom. I saw you going down the hall." He hesitated in thought a moment. "I saw someone tall walking down the hall."

I smiled again. "I saw that same figure last night."

Michael raised an eyebrow. "That's weird."

"I know," I said.

Michael shook his head and went to his bedroom.

By Sunday night, I'd reached the point that my neck was hurting from jerking it to the side so much, trying to catch a glimpse of our ethereal visitor. I knew someone was trying to get our attention.

Heather had taken her bath and was getting ready for bed when I tapped on her door. She opened it and had a disturbed look on her face. When I came in, I sat down on the bottom bunk of her bed and asked her what was wrong. She hesitated, started brushing her long, brown hair, and sighed.

"Well," she began, "Apollo is acting weird. . .and. . ."

I looked down at our gray striped tabby, Apollo, and wondered what Heather considered "weird." The cat had acted abnormal since we got her for my birthday in June. I had named her Apollo after the medicine god in Greek Mythology who supposedly taught humans how to heal themselves. I was into understanding the healing aspect of my spirituality at the time and knew that our family could use a little help in the healing department. My son, Rusty, had several food allergies, atopic dermatitis, and asthma. He was also allergic to cats. We had given away a different tabby many years before because an asthma attack had sent Rusty to the hospital, and the doctor urged us to get rid of any allergens that could bring on another attack. It was a frightening time for our whole family because Rusty almost died. So without hesitation, we gave away our very well behaved tabby. The other children suffered the loss, and later we realized that giving the tabby away caused more harm to Rusty than keeping her.

16

Six years later, we took the chance of bringing another cat into our home; to rectify the trauma that had occurred earlier, but Apollo was one strange behaving kitten. So when Heather told me that she was acting weird, I wasn't alarmed. Yet, what she told me next did alarm me.

"Mom," Heather began softly, "I just saw a guy in my room. He was walking out of my closet. When I looked again, he was gone."

So that's why Apollo was acting different. *She* had seen him, too. Years before, I had read that cats had psychic abilities, including being able to see apparitions.

Heather stood waiting for my reaction.

"Michael and I have seen him, too," I said.

She sighed with relief. "Good, but, Mom, I'm getting a different feeling about him. Kind of sad."

I nodded. "Me, too."

"It's not like when I saw Pawpaw." She smiled as she remembered her grandfather who had died in a car accident seven years before. "When I saw Pawpaw walking out of the closet, he made me smile."

"Not the first time you saw him," I reminded her.

We both giggled. The first time she had seen my father in her room, she didn't smile. Smiling was the last thing on her mind. It was about six months after my father had died and I had been sitting on the sofa with Bob when suddenly I turned to him and said, "I need to check on Heather."

I had already kissed her goodnight but felt this strange pull to her room. When I reached her bedroom, I found her hiding beneath the covers, trembling in terror. It wasn't easy explaining to a six-year-old that dead grandparents can still come by for a visit, and they don't have to use the front door anymore.

Suddenly her pretty green eyes lit up. "Hey, maybe you can ask about this guy in your psychic class next week."

I smiled at her enthusiasm. "I guess I should. I have a feeling that he's going to be around for a while."

Heather nodded. "Me, too."

I kissed her goodnight and closed the door behind me.

17

As I walked down the hall, I wondered why this young man had come to our home and allowed himself to be seen by three different people.

Over the course of the next few months, we learned that he had been with us for quite some time.

We had just missed the signs.

I asked Edgar how he was able to allow me to see him when he appeared that night in my home. Here was his reply:

In the energy source we have a great multitude of choices. We are given so much to work with because we know what is available. In time, many centuries from now, all will be able to see the different levels of existence. When in the afterlife, we are shown all that is. And so with that we are able to bring forth what is needed at this time. If you were to have introduced the computer systems in the 1800's it would have been incomprehensible because they knew not of the technology that is available today. It is so with us in being able to use the source to our advantage. There is life after life in all circumstances. All. The body is physical and made up of atoms in which is used until the mind has found use to destroy it, or perhaps the spirit has accomplished what it has come to do. But the soul is a continuous life form, everlasting as Jesus knew it to be that is why he feared not his death, but knew there was the afterlife.

Chapter Three

Finding a Piece that Fits

The following Thursday night, I went to the class on spirituality that I had been attending for over a year. During the class, the teacher would give us channeled information in which we could apply to our daily lives and our spiritual journey. Before the class began, I sat talking with the other ladies and had completely forgotten about the young spirit whom I had witnessed in my home.

About an hour later when the teacher came to me, she said, ". . .It has come through to us that you have a great quality of life left. Try to understand there is a soul on this side who meets you in the desert. He wears a cap on the back of his head with the bill of the hat turned back. He's a young man. He looks like he needs a shave, but whoever he is he's a wonderful person. He's coming to our world, but he will come back into your world to help you with the communication skills that you must work on. He's going to make you listen to him whether you want to or not. He says he's like a cow that just keeps chewing. He will never give up. He says you hear him like an ache in your heart at times. He's not harmful. He's a participant of your world, but he grew into life very quickly. He took his life, and now he's going to heal himself by working with you upon this earth. He wants to learn how to live again, and you can help him do that. You're going to grow hungrier. You're going to find yourself nourishing more of yourself than is needed and even though this may sound weird to you, I guarantee you in the spring of the year you're going to feel the impact of him. He has a greater quality of words than you, and he is much more creative in his mind than you are. He comes to help you as well as your helping him. He says, you can call him Edgar."

I sat there stunned, a bit shaken and wondering what in the world was going on, but I immediately *knew* he was the young man that my children and I had seen in our home.

The teacher went on to the next person as I waited quite impatiently for the part of the class that allowed us to ask follow-up questions. My mind raced. A young man in our home? This statement made our perceptions real. There was no longer the option to discard the apparition as a figment of our imaginations. I had not mentioned our viewing Edgar to anyone prior to the class. Only my family members were aware of our new visitor.

Edgar wanted to be acknowledged. He had a purpose. I was intrigued and yet a bit frightened all at once.

Finally during the last half hour of the class, we were allowed to ask questions. I raised my hand nervously, all the while debating whether I wanted to know or not know about my new acquaintance.

"My great-grandfather's name was Edgar, but he didn't commit suicide . . .and we've seen a young man in our home recently. Why did he pick that name?"

I was told that Edgar chose that name so we would think of him in love, as we would love a grandfather and so we would be comfortable with him in our presence.

Then the teacher added one more thing. "He is showing me a piece of white paper. Like sheet paper flying through the air. It's coming through and around the fireplace."

I thanked her for the information then she moved onto the other questions.

Paper flying through the air? I wondered what that was about, though I didn't question it further. I was still trying to absorb the previous information. In the past, when my mother and father had died and appeared to me briefly, I was usually surprised, yet also comforted in knowing they were okay. This was an entirely different feeling. This young man was a stranger to me. He had no intentions of leaving and had decided to take up residence in my home. I was nervous yet excited. I loved mysteries when they were in book form or a video, because when I became impatient, I could read the back of the book and find out the outcome or forward it to the end of the movie to see how it ended. But this was different. I had to wait to find out why he had come to my home. Why he chose me to help him. And why he thought I could heal him.

On the drive home, I tried to convince myself that it was all a coincidence and that none of it was true. I did believe in the afterlife since I had already experienced proof many times with my own relatives, but that was at my convenience. Now I had been placed in a situation that no longer allowed me to pick and choose what I wanted to believe in. So, by nature I fought the circumstances by denying the truth.

Once I got home, I walked in the back door fully prepared to share with my daughter what I had learned and ready to conclude that it was purely coincidental. I had also prepared a "we don't have to believe in this if we choose not to" speech.

When I reached the living room, I realized my choices were no longer there. Heather and Rusty were giggling exceptionally loud. On the floor below them and covering the fireplace hearth were numerous paper airplanes. *Paper flying through the air . . .around the fireplace.*

Edgar's words replayed in my head. At that moment I knew he was aware of what was going on in my home even while I was away, and that he would make me listen, whether I wanted to or not.

I asked Edgar why he came into my world when he did. Here was his reply:

As on the physical plane you seek out teachers to guide and lead you to higher learning for the future, the spiritual world does the same. We were introduced in a form that would be the most productive to humanity. When one reaches our side they realize that all humans are working together for a purpose. It is not for a self-centered action but for the good of the whole.

We come to your world to show you what is needed in the physical plane to better understand the spiritual plane. We knew that you would be able to connect with the children because of your deep love of children. Your empathic nature brings to you the gain that is needed to focus on helping those who are on your side.

Just as you are given the forecast for the weather a week in advance, we are given the forecast for the future occurrences lifetimes before. We know what needs to be done and we find the correct manner of accomplishing it. You were chosen to be taught in a time when the percentage of the population was beginning to open their eyes to other possibilities. A microwave oven would not have been created before there was electricity.

Our manner of teaching is such. We look for students who will be the best placed in the circumstances that are presented. We find who will try to work for humanity and put their ego aside. On the physical level, that is not an easy task. Whenever the ego appears, the sacrifices for humanity disappear.

Chapter Four

The Background Begins to Take Form

Days passed and I found myself being led to discover new pieces of the puzzle. Everywhere I turned, looked or listened, I heard the words German or Germany. The previous summer, I had registered for a course on how to speak German, not having a clue as to why I was doing so. I attended one class, bought the book that the instructor recommended, and never returned. However, I did study the book quite frequently. I was interested in the language and enjoyed the pronunciation of the words. It just seemed so natural.

Weeks after I had learned about Edgar, I noticed there was some sort of German connection that he was trying to make me understand. There were just too many coincidences surrounding the words German and Germany that were being brought to my attention. Even Heather began noticing it after she had chosen the book *The Diary of Anne Frank* to read for a report at school.

One afternoon as the holidays grew near, I was scanning a catalog, making a list of the foods and treats that I was going to order as gifts for my family and friends. In the catalog, I noticed an angel trinket box. The angel was holding a star. I couldn't stop looking at it. It was so cute, so simple. I considered ordering it for myself, but then decided against it. I never thought of it again.

Two weeks later when the package arrived with the food, I began unloading it from the large box and into my refrigerator. I came across a box that read, Angel Treasure Box.

I stared at it a moment and tried to remember if I had ordered it after all, but I just knew that I hadn't. I opened the little white box and inside was the angel holding the star I had seen in the catalog. I kept shaking my head saying, no, no, no. I did not order this.

I located the invoice, but it did not list the treasure box. I called the company and told them what happened and asked them if I had ordered it by mistake. They checked their order form and it was not listed. The lady told me not to worry about it. There was no record of it anywhere.

When I hung up, I heard someone say, "Merry Christmas."

Looking around, I got a chill. I was the only one in the house at the time. Then I smiled to myself. Could Edgar have done this?

So, I said aloud, "Edgar, if this is from you, give me another confirmation. I'm not that easily convinced."

Then I heard him say, "Go to the drug store and you will find a Christmas card that is written in German."

I thought, sure I will, but decided to challenge him. I had a little time left before I had to pick up my children from school, so I left early and headed toward Walgreen's. Just as I tried to turn in the driveway, a car cut me off and I was forced to go into another lane. The traffic prevented me from making my turn and I ended up driving farther down the road. I turned into the parking lot adjacent from Walgreen's so that I could make a U-turn. I then noticed the Eckerd's drug store in that parking lot and decided to go there instead.

When I went inside, I went straight to the greeting cards and said to Edgar silently but also sarcastically, "Okay, show me this German card."

Right in front of me was indeed a Christmas card written in German. I stood there dumbfounded for a moment. I had never seen one like that before in this town, nor in my whole life, and it was the only one of its kind on the rack. I checked. Quite humbly I told Edgar, "Okay, I'm convinced."

But, being the skeptical person that I am, I left Eckerd's and drove to Walgreen's, went inside and checked the greeting cards. There were no German cards there. Edgar made sure that I reached the right store and got the confirmation I needed, even if it took a careless driver to do so. He was indeed teaching me about communication. That was my first lesson in learning to trust his voice in my experiences.

The next week, I couldn't wait to share my story with the class. When it was my turn, I asked, "Is Edgar German and what message does he have for me tonight?"

The teacher took a deep breath, sighed and then began. "He likes to be that of the spy. He's enjoying the mystery of this creation. He has a German approach to life as you do. He may link back to a German incarnation, but he just likes the air of creation that it forms. It is our passage with him that he's linking with, and it was in that time period that you made a connection. If you look back in those periods of time in which Germans found the earth, they were given great authority within their own abundance. Edgar is the person who is giving to you this insight. Their techniques of thought were very simplistic. He's there to help you stay simple within yourself. But more importantly, he's there to help you multiply and grow. He wants you to start tasting the salt of another's face. He wants you to start listening to the pain that they create, but he also wants you to look at the funnel of knowledge that is given through the emotion. Then you can understand the power of the thought that you create. He's there. He's just loving the opportunity to shower you with his time. Enjoy his presence."

I was pleased the teacher gave me so much information, but trying to process it all at once was difficult. I was glad the classes were taped so I could go back and listen to the information again later. The only thing that stood out in my mind that night were the two phrases, "he's there to help you multiply and grow" and ". . .wants you to start tasting the salt of another's face." I had no idea what Edgar meant by those statements.

Months passed as Edgar continually made his presence known in our home. Heather and I received signs from him quite regularly and always with German as the significant factor. Later, we began to notice that the word "suicide" was being brought to our attention. It was quite frightening when we first noticed it. We didn't know if it meant that someone in our family or someone we knew would be attempting suicide. But soon it became the common link of communication through Edgar. Once again, there were too many coincidences containing that subject being presented to us all at once.

One day in April, I was cleaning the house and suddenly became extremely exhausted. I felt the need to lie down right away. I went to the loveseat and stretched out. I was only asleep for a short time, but I dreamed that a young girl was being taken away by strangers in black coats. When I woke up, it seemed so real that I wasn't sure if I had dreamed it or if I had heard about it somewhere.

Later that evening, when I went back to sit on the loveseat to watch television, I began recalling the dream. The moment it popped into my mind, the pendulum on the clock above the fireplace began banging forward instead of swinging back and forth. It was loud and got my attention. It continued to do that for a minute as I watched it clanging. Michael, my oldest son, walked in and the pendulum stopped banging forward and went back to its perpetual motion. I stared at the clock for a moment then asked him, "Could you step out of the room for a moment?"

He shrugged but did as I asked.

The pendulum began banging forward again.

I motioned for him to come back and then pointed at the clock. He saw what it was doing, raised an eyebrow, and then the pendulum went back to normal. He shook his head, stepped up onto the fireplace hearth and readjusted the pendulum. "It must be the air conditioner making it do that."

I nodded but was not completely convinced. The air conditioner had been running for days and the pendulum had never done that. Edgar was trying to get my attention, and I believed it had something to do with my dream, though I decided to keep that to myself.

32

The next day when I woke my daughter for school, she shuddered as her gaze focused on something behind me. She shut her eyes tightly then reopened them.

"What's wrong?" I asked.

"I just saw two guys standing behind you in black trench coats," she said, still looking behind me. "Then they disappeared."

Naturally, I turned around to see what could have caused that reaction from her. All I saw was an empty wall. I still didn't mention my dream.

"Maybe, it was part of a dream and you aren't awake completely," I tried to assure her.

She shook her head adamantly. "No, they were here. And they were scary."

I left the room wondering what Edgar was trying to tell me. I just couldn't figure it out.

A few nights later, the answering machine picked up, though I had not heard the phone ringing. I checked the phone and the ringer was on. I then checked the caller ID, and it was Michael's cell phone number. He was in his bedroom, so I went there and knocked on the door, all the time wondering why he would be calling me from his bedroom. When I opened the door to his room, I saw that he was lying on the bed watching a movie, his cell phone across the room on his dresser. I asked him why he called our number until the answering machine picked up, and he said he hadn't touched his phone in hours. It didn't make sense. I could only believe Edgar was saying that I still wasn't hearing what he was trying to tell me. I wasn't "getting the message."

Then on April 20th, our cat's birthday, Apollo went mad. It was late afternoon, and the children had already gotten home from school.

Heather came into the kitchen where I was and said, "Mom, something's wrong with Apollo."

I cringed. Something was always wrong with Apollo. We had never had a cat that had as many problems as that one. "What do you mean?" I asked, not really wanting to know.

"Well, she's trying to climb my bedroom walls," Heather began. "And she's running up and down the hall like she's being chased."

"Kittens do that. She's just getting her energy out."

Heather shook her head unconvinced. "No, something's wrong with her. She's bowing up and hissing, and her eyes don't look right."

I left the kitchen and went into the living room. There was Apollo, racing down the hall and smacking into the baseboard. She jumped upward as if she were trying to catch something on the wall.

I checked for shadows, assuming that maybe she was being teased by them. There were none.

Apollo continued this strange behavior for hours. By late evening she finally settled down. Heather came out of her room with a sad look on her face.

"What's wrong?" I asked.

"Don't you feel it?" she asked in return.

"Feel what?"

"The sadness in here. Mom, it's everywhere. It's like something bad is getting ready to happen. It's just so sad."

I had felt the sadness earlier, but thought it was my own feeling of knowing that something was wrong with Apollo and wondering if we were going to have to find a new home for her, too.

Heather looked at me. "I think it has to do with Edgar. He's trying to tell us something."

"Do you think he's sad?"

"Yes. And I think he is the one who was making Apollo act crazy."

It made sense. But why would he be sad? And what was he trying to tell us concerning Apollo?

Later that evening, we learned about the tragedy at Columbine High School.

" . . .*in the spring of next year you will feel the impact of him.*"

34

This was Edgar's first lesson to us on how to pay attention to the signs. April 20th was Apollo's birthday. It was also a famous German's birthday: Hitler. The boys from Columbine High School committed suicide on that day. They were also wearing black trench coats and had killed a young girl. We were given many pieces to the puzzle yet we had no idea how to connect them.

Edgar had tried to open the door of communication with us. Unfortunately, we were too new at it to understand his method. It was like learning a foreign language from a foreigner. Quite an interesting challenge and at the same time also very confusing.

Heather and I learned many things that day. We learned to pay attention to the repetition of a circumstance, a name or a situation. We also learned that we needed to pay attention to our emotions. Perhaps it was his way of showing us what he felt . . .*he wants you to start tasting the salt of another's face . . .he wants you to look at the funnel of knowledge that is given through the emotions.*

I believe he knew what was going to happen that day, and he was trying to make us understand.

From that moment forward, we learned to pay attention to the signs.

I asked Edgar what happens to the children who commit suicide. Here was his reply:

When a child reaches the point of no return and finds their only solace is in taking his own life, then once he comes to our side, we take him to a place of healing. He must view his experiences and note how they could have turned out if he were to finish his entirety in the physical. We show him where he has taken the wrong path and what led him to it. We show him what he could have done to change his circumstances and therefore proceeded on his life's path. We show him the opportunities that he missed had he waited just a while longer during his learning experience. We show him that nothing is so bad that cannot be resolved on the physical plane.

When a child comes to this side from suicide, they are suffering a depression that takes much time to heal. They must learn what it is like to reacquaint themselves with the spirit for they have lost touch with their soul's path. Sometimes before coming to the physical plane, a soul will go with great expectations of what is to come and what they can accomplish.

Unfortunately, the road sometimes becomes bumpier than they had prepared for and they realize that it is not the lifetime in which they had presumed. It becomes difficult for them to accept the challenges that they have given themselves and in their physical heart they feel as if they have failed. Unless there is another spiritual being who is in the same place of lingering and truly understands this soul, the soul becomes weak and chooses not to stay and fulfill his mission. Therefore, there is much healing that must be done before he may return again.

It is of a different place that the child reaches when they have taken their own life. Of course, it is not a bad place, but a place where they must relearn what they have already learned and try once again to understand what brought them to that point. Some children think that if they take their own life that the suffering will be over. But, they will only be reaching us in the same frame of mind that they left with and will still have to deal with what wasn't dealt with while in the physical. The feelings are still the same for the individual that is why they come across to their parents with recognizable traits.

Chapter Five

Interlocking Pieces

Several days later, I had a routine doctor's appointment. I sat in a chair, waiting for the doctor to come in. I began thinking about the suicides that had occurred earlier in the week. Suddenly the paper on the examining table crinkled as if someone had kicked it. I glanced at it and thought it was the air conditioner blowing it. About a minute later, I began thinking about the suicides again and how Edgar had tried to get my attention with the pendulum on the clock. The paper crinkled and moved again. By then I knew it was not the air conditioner. So, just as a test, I waited to see if it would happen a third time, but it didn't. I then resumed thinking about the suicides, and the paper crinkled again. This time I caught a glimpse out of the corner of my eye of a young man sitting on the table. His foot was hanging where the paper was appearing to be kicked. I turned my head quickly to see him completely, but he vanished.

Shortly afterwards, the doctor walked in. He wore a look of concern on his face. Instead of his usual hello, he stared at me. "Are you all right?" he asked.

I nodded slowly. "Yes, why?"

He stared at me. "Your face is very pale."

I wanted to say, "Oh, I just saw a ghost," but instead I said, "I was just thinking about the tragedy that happened in Colorado."

At that moment, the lights dimmed in the room for a long moment, then returned to normal. The doctor raised an eyebrow and I just shrugged. I realized by that time that Edgar wasn't only hanging out at my home, he was everywhere I was, regardless of the situation. It was then that I asked him to present himself in a more subtle form.

41

A month later, Edgar taught me a new way to let me know when he was around. It was late afternoon, and I needed to pick up my children from school. I also needed to stop at the grocery store beforehand. The nearest grocery store is about a mile from my home, yet for some reason I felt compelled to go to the grocery store that was eight miles away. I kept thinking I needed to go there for something, though I didn't know what. When I reached the store, I immediately had the feeling I would run into Judy Collier, a lady who took the spirituality class with me. I hadn't seen her since the class ended in February.

Over two years before, when I had first met Judy, she was in deep grief over the loss of her son, Kyle. Though her loss was tragic, she had an energy about her that charged the room. I enjoyed the stories she shared with the class about her after death communications with Kyle. I had lost my father several years before and had similar experiences. So hearing her stories reinforced my belief that what I had experienced was real.

Upon entering the store, I went straight to the freezer isle and there she stood. I walked up to her. We hugged and exchanged pleasantries. I told her I rarely shopped in that store and never when I needed to pick up my kids from school because it was out of my way to do so.

At that moment a gnat appeared, swarming around my eyes. I didn't know where it had come from and could not seem to get rid of it. Then it flew over to Judy and she swatted at it. We started laughing because it was being such a pest as we tried to talk. The freezer aisle just didn't seem like the place to find a gnat, unlike the produce department.

Immediately I heard Edgar say, "It's me."

I just smiled at Judy as we talked and because we were both in a hurry, we cut our conversation short and went our separate ways vowing to keep in touch.

After buying the groceries and rushing home, I kept hearing Edgar talk to me. He was urging me to get to my computer. Quickly, I put away the groceries and sat down to type whatever it was he wanted to say to me.

That is when something new happened. It was no longer Edgar talking to me. It was Kyle, Judy's son.

Edgar had led me to the grocery store for Kyle's sake. Kyle had a message for his mother that he wanted relayed, and he knew I would do it.

I listened as Kyle dictated the letter to his mother. His main concern was for her to tell everyone about her experiences with the afterlife. He knew she was capable and a wonderful speaker. He showed me an image of her shouting her information from the mountaintops to others in need.

I typed up the information, printed it out and quickly put it in an envelope and addressed it to Judy. I felt I had to get it to her as soon as possible, but I was a bit hesitant to do so. I had never taken it for granted that people wanted messages from their loved ones on the Other Side. I was very leery of forcing my channeled communication on anyone. I was still a bit skeptical of it myself so how could I expect anyone to believe what I was hearing? Yet I kept feeling that this was important and that I needed to trust what I heard. I asked for further confirmation that this was the right thing to do.

Instead of putting it in the mailbox for the next day's mail to be picked up, I was shown that I needed to drive to the post office to drop it off. I knew I was pressed for time and I needed to pick up my children from school in fifteen minutes. But I kept hearing, "Trust."

So I did. Later down the road, while riding in my van, the radio came on by itself. I had always played tapes and never listened to the radio. So when it came on, I was a bit surprised. Before I turned it off, I heard a Rod Stewart song begin playing. It was "Forever Young." Then I got an image of Kyle. He was 26 when he was killed in a car accident. I realized that was the confirmation that I was truly connecting with him. I dropped off the letter and went on to pick up my children from school with plenty of time to spare. If I had not driven out of my way, I would not have had the opportunity to hear that song. Edgar and Kyle knew that if I were on the road long enough, I would be able to receive their confirmation. That is why it was important for me not to mail the letter from my home.

The next day, Judy called me after receiving my letter. She was excited to hear that Kyle had communicated through me. She was even more excited when she learned that he was approving of her newest endeavor. She had decided to write a book about her experiences, though she had never mentioned it to me.

During our conversation, I mentioned to Judy that my van radio came on with the song, "Forever Young" playing and asked her if that song had any significance to her.

She became silent a moment then said, "Jim and I were just talking last night about how we will always think of Kyle as being forever young because he died when he was twenty-six."

I glanced at my window as she said that and noticed a gnat swarming around the pane. I mentally thanked Edgar for bringing Kyle to me so I could give this message to his mother. It validated the information I had given to her previously concerning her book.

That was the day I learned that Edgar had chosen to appear as a gnat so I would not be shaken upon seeing him as an apparition. It is much easier to accept a spirit as something small and harmless than to be shown an image of a person in an instant. The apparition tends to be frightening at times, and yet other times I find myself trying to look for it again. The gnat was humorous to me, and I could easily accept it. He taught me much that day in the form of communication, but the most important thing was that the spirit world tries hard to communicate in ways that are the most comfortable to us. That is how important it is to them to get their messages across. Little did I know this small incidence was the day that Kyle had volunteered to become leader of the pack of the children who came to me for healing. It was almost a year later before I learned of Kyle's and Edgar's plans for me.

I asked Kyle how he was able to bring the animals to me. Here was his reply:

The Other Side brings to us the energies of all living things. A true paradise for me. I am able to bring to you the animals because they are aware of my existence in the energy realm just as they were while I was on your side. I feel the existence of nature because it is a part of who I am. I enjoy the closest parts of nature because it shows the God energy in all things.

Life on our side is very much like life on your side. However the animals of nature are more in tune with us than you are. Why? It is a God given blessing because that is their instincts. Why do birds gather food before cold weather approaches? Why do animals hide beneath objects before a tornado hits? Why do the sounds of the creatures in the physical life become silent before a natural disaster? Because they are in tune with the existence of the greater forces.

Over here, as Edgar has said, we are much more able to see what is available to us. We know where you are going to be and when, because at given times, not always though, we are able to fast forward to what needs to be done. We see the picture before you do. We get the premier version. Then we use our input to be able to get messages through to you.

I will give you an example that will apply to all who are interested. Suppose you were going to go to a sporting event. You buy your tickets ahead of time and know where you are going to sit. You allow for a certain amount of time to get there, to be there, to leave from there. You plan it out to a certain degree. But you don't know how the game will go, who will make the best plays and which team will win. We do. So given the fact that we are able to see the end of the game before it is played, we see the opportunities to present the signs that are needed to get your attention at the correct moment. We are not always given the entire picture. Only the times when it is best applied to what we need to accomplish. We are all here with our own agendas. We apply what we can to guide those who we need to.

I bring animals to you when the opportunity arises. All of God's creatures are a part of the bigger picture. They willingly allow themselves to play a vital role in the spiritual growth of the planet. Appreciate them for they are the most humble messengers.

Chapter Six

No Longer Fully Interlocking Pieces

During the summer, I found myself being led to buy many new CDs. I began to think Edgar was having a good time shopping with me. I felt his presence constantly. The first CD he encouraged me to buy was called, *Back In the High Life* by Steve Winwood. I had always enjoyed his music, so buying another one of his CDs was not an unusual thing for me. But one night while taking a bubble bath, something unusual happened concerning that particular CD.

I had lit a vanilla scented candle and filled the tub with bubbles. I brought the remote control with me so I could listen to the music as I relaxed. I thought maybe that I would find a few new songs I liked. When I turned the CD player on, the first song that played was "Higher Love." I closed my eyes, relaxed and enjoyed the scent of the vanilla candle as the music played.

Time passed as I listened to the next five songs. But as the sixth song played, it got noticeably louder. I assumed it was just the quality of the recording. I turned it down with the remote. I didn't pay much attention to the words, just enjoyed the beat.

When the song was over, it replayed itself again. I assumed I had hit the repeat button when I tried to turn it down, so I forwarded it to the next song. But it wouldn't go forward. It continued to play the same song. I worked with the remote control for several minutes and finally gave up.

Then I said aloud, "Okay, Edgar, you have my attention. What's going on?"

The song continued to play and repeat itself until I turned it off completely.

Later that evening when I went back into the bedroom, I passed the CD player and just out of curiosity, I pressed the play button on the remote and the sixth song came on first. I

49

found the CD case and looked up the name of the song because I had never heard it before. It was called "Wake Me Up on Judgment Day." I realized that was not a coincidence so I found a piece of paper and a pen and listened to the song, writing down the lyrics.

The one verse that got my attention was "Say a prayer for the stranger. Listen to the stranger." As I listened to the song over and over I realized that much of the song related to Edgar's presence in my life.

Suddenly I felt compassion for this young stranger and realized that he had much to say, if only I could learn how to listen. That night, I realized his favorite method of communication: through songs.

My oldest son had taken an interest in the Doors' music during that time and since I could usually hear it through his bedroom wall, I became accustomed to hearing it and decided I liked it. Edgar must have liked it also because I began noticing it on the radio of my car at the same time I received a message from him. Then not long after, my son bought the movie, *The Doors*, and I watched it, feeling some strange connection to Jim Morrison. I kept thinking Edgar was trying to get my attention concerning the movie. I watched it over and over to try to understand what it was that he was trying to tell me. But I could never put the pieces together to mean anything that seemed significant to my life.

That's when the spiders began appearing. I started noticing spiders everywhere I was throughout the house. Though they did not frighten me, they did seem to follow me. If I were in my bedroom searching for something, there would be a spider climbing on the window screen. When I went into the kitchen and began to cook, I noticed a similar sized spider on my kitchen windowsill. If I returned to the bedroom, the other spider would be gone. I could not understand the connection. But the spiders seemed to follow me and yet, they didn't bother me.

One morning I woke up from a very strange dream and when I opened my eyes, there was a spider directly above my head on the ceiling. I knew it was a message for me to pay attention to my dreams. But I remember thinking, "this is getting ridiculous!"

But Edgar did get my attention with the spider above my head. Enough so that I tried to figure out what dream it was that he wanted me to acknowledge. I have always had prophetic dreams and the previous year Michael had given me a dream journal for Christmas. I had recorded my dreams quite regularly in the book trying to understand their meanings in my life.

That day I found the dream journal and began searching through the pages. On the page that was dated April 27, 1998, over a year before, I had dreamed I was moving into a mobile home and I was clearing out everything. During one part of the dream I was talking to a young guy. I knew he was upset about a death. He broke down in tears and hung his head. I told him it was okay, that I would help him and that I understood his pain. Then I woke up.

As I read the page, I realized it had been Edgar that I had seen in my dream. He had come to me in the dream, and on a spiritual level I had agreed to help him. Only until November of that year did he feel comfortable enough to appear in my home. When I had dreamt that dream, it had meant nothing because I didn't recognize the person, nor did it make sense to me. But as time passed I learned that dreaming about a different home referred to the idea of moving into a new way of thought. And accepting Edgar into my life was definitely moving into a new way of thought. In many ways!

Later during the summer, I found myself enjoying the Doors' music so much that Michael bought their CD as my birthday gift. All the while, I was still trying to connect the music with the spider. It made no sense, and I was really becoming frustrated at the puzzle that I was being given. One day while going through some magazines, I noticed a spider crawling right over my hand. I slung it down and said aloud, "Okay Spiderman, what is it?" Then I thought, "Wait, Spiderman? Maybe there is something to that . . ."

51

So, as luck would have it, since my youngest son, Rusty, was interested in collecting cards I suggested a trip to the nearest cards and comics store. There I searched through boxes of Spiderman Comics trying to figure out the message that Edgar was trying to relay to me. Finally when nothing really seemed to click, I picked three comics by chance and decided to buy them. But once I got home that day, circumstances prevented me from being able to further investigate the comics and they were put aside for days.

A week passed before I had the opportunity to look through them. But nothing ever seemed to apply to what was happening in my life. It was years later before Heather ever connected the misshapen pieces.

I asked Edgar why he came to me in a dream much earlier than before it was time for me to work with him. Here was his reply:

In preparation for a trip, one must plan, pack and map out the destiny. It is no different in the life of a human spirit on the physical plane. It was important that I came to you when you were not expecting. It is proof that you would have sought after later.

Let me give you an example. Before you plan a vacation, you must choose a place to go. Then you will call about a place to stay. Next you will plan what you will bring and where you will go once you reach the destination. All of this is done in advance. It makes the vacation run smoother if there is preparation going into it beforehand.

In order to lead you on your path, there needed to be a map. A plan. A destination. Had I appeared and told you that you were going to be a medium for deceased children you would have first been frightened then scoffed at me. Possibly even believed you had hallucinated the entire thing.

Therefore I have been guided to lead you in the best direction that would bring to you the most learning. You would not go through New York to get to California from Florida. That would be out of your way, make for a long and tiresome experience and the learning would be lost. I knew your destination from the beginning. I had to come to you in a dream to prepare you for the possibilities. Would you buy a motorcycle for a child who hadn't yet learned to sit on a tricycle?

Chapter Seven

Building the Border of the Puzzle

The summer passed, and I found myself trying to understand Edgar's presence in my life. I realized he was teaching me to communicate. But why? I admit I enjoyed his games and mysteries. I've always been one who had to know why things happened. Rarely do I accept that they just happen. So I spent much of my time wondering why he was there and what he intended to do once I learned how to communicate with him. What was our purpose? I questioned him repeatedly about this.

Then I received a call from Judy Collier. She had completed her book and asked if I would help her edit it. I had been writing short stories, novels and screenplays for over ten years, but when my mother became sick with cancer I put my writing aside. After she died in January of 1997, I never returned to it. So getting back to the writing life was exciting to me even if I weren't the one writing. I agreed to meet with Judy at her house the following day.

I was looking forward to meeting with Judy because she is such a lively upbeat person. Even after her only son died, she was able to pick herself back up and find life after death. I have always admired her strength and stamina so when she asked me to edit her book, I was glad to be visiting with her on a regular basis again. I had begun to miss our Thursday night classes and the stories each other shared.

The next day I parked in front of her house and sat there for a moment. I asked Kyle and Edgar to bring to me confirmation that they would be with me. I looked around hoping for a sign. I listened to the radio and nothing seemed to strike me as a message. Then I saw a large black crow fly over. During our Thursday night class, Judy had often mentioned that Kyle let her know he was around by bringing squirrels, raccoons, or black crows into her sight. So I said, "Okay, boys."

Once she invited me in, I felt Kyle's presence. I had never been to her house before, but I realized that he had indeed joined us.

Then I heard him say, "Ask her about the problem she had this morning putting in her right earring."

I waited a moment, debating whether or not I should tell her this. Even though I knew Judy was very open to spiritual communication this was still difficult. After all, he was her dearly loved son. Could I take the chance of telling her something that I had heard and it possibly not be true?

Judy led me into the kitchen and I sat down at her dining table. I stared at her a moment and finally said, "Kyle wants me to ask you about the problem you had putting in your right earring this morning."

Judy stared at me. I immediately thought, "Oh no. I've misunderstood what he was saying."

"I did have trouble," she said and went on to explain that it took her many tries before she was able to finally hit the hole with the post.

She shook her head smiling. "So is Kyle here with us?"

I mentally thanked Kyle for giving me correct information. "Yes. He's very excited that I am helping you with your book." I could feel his joy as we spoke and the energy that he displayed while in the room with us. I glanced at the dining room window and noticed several squirrels had gathered. More signs from Kyle. From that day on, I learned to notice the animals appearing on a daily basis. When playing charades with the spirit world, I discovered they use what they are associated with and what is most convenient to the situation. Living in south Louisiana, I couldn't expect Kyle to bring a camel or elephant into my view regularly, but a squirrel was more likely. The challenge then became to decipher when it was a sign or a coincidence. I learned later that after entering the door to the spirit world with eyes wide open, there are no coincidences. Only messages that have been misinterpreted.

I met with Judy several more times and Kyle always joined us with his input for her book, *Quit Kissing My Ashes*. Even the title was his idea. Judy had previously given it a title that she found to be generic and decided that she wanted to change it. So one day while sitting at her dining table, we brainstormed with our own thoughts for a new title. Nothing really appealed to either of us.

Finally, I heard Kyle say, "Ask her about what she was told about me once."

By that time I trusted Kyle's voice in my world, so I relayed that to her.

She shrugged and shook her head. She didn't know what he meant.

Kyle then told me, "The part about the ashes." So I told her what he said.

She looked at me kind of funny and laughed. "You mean the part about quit kissing my ashes?"

Kyle immediately showed me a "thumbs up" image. I knew she had hit on what he was trying to tell her.

I said, "Yes. That's it. That's what he wants the title to be."

She laughed again with her wonderful contagious laugh.

Suddenly, we both got sort of giggly and agreed the title should be something people would remember. It would reflect the humor that is displayed throughout the book.

Several months passed and I continued to help her with her book. I was basically retyping the manuscript and putting it into book form. I could always feel Kyle around me while I worked. He often gave me signs as confirmations. The screen of the monitor would become blurred, then suddenly clear up. Or the cursor would fly all over the screen. Words would get deleted and no matter how many times I retyped them, they would end up gone once I printed out the material to bring to Judy. I knew Kyle had decided to edit it himself. Judy and I could only joke about it. How else could it be explained?

At times as I sat at my computer and retyped the chapters, I could feel tickling across the back of my neck. Sometimes it was so often that I would put my hair in a ponytail to keep it from annoying me. One day after typing, I noticed red marks on my neck from where I had been rubbing it all afternoon.

A few days later, Judy told me she had been to a weekend lecture with our former teacher. When she asked her if Kyle were around me while I worked on her book, the teacher told her, "Yes, he even plays with her hair while she types, tickling the back of her neck."

That was confirmation for me that I wasn't just creating these images in my mind and stretching the circumstances to fit the situation. Kyle was there. And I knew it!

After much time spent communicating with Kyle while reading his experiences, I found that without thinking, some of the most profound thoughts would come to me as I typed. When Judy would give me a new chapter to enter into the computer, I would first type it without editing, just mainly trying to put it on a file so that I could go back and edit it when I was alone and able to concentrate. During many of these typing sessions, I kept hearing Kyle say that I needed to help the children. Of course, I was at a loss about "what children." I couldn't understand what he meant. At first I thought he meant my own. So I would check on them, see they were all right and then go back to typing.

One day it dawned on me that he meant the children on the Other Side. I decided to question Judy about it and see what she thought. She was happy to do whatever Kyle suggested and knew that it would bring other mothers comfort just as she had received when getting messages from Kyle.

In March, she called some friends who had also lost children and invited them to her house. I was a little nervous in the beginning because I had never held a group reading for grieving mothers. Previously, I had practiced and fine-tuned my abilities with a small group of friends who had trusted me enough to experiment on them each Wednesday night for almost a year, but those ladies weren't gathered to hear from their deceased children. They were open to whatever messages I received from anyone, be it their spirit guides, their angels, or their deceased relatives.

So as I sat there wondering just how I was going to call up specific children for their mothers, fears and doubts raced through my mind. What if no one shows up from the spirit world? What if I can't hear or see anything for these ladies?

Once the meeting began, I mentally asked Edgar and Kyle to give me some sort of affirmation that I was doing the right thing. That's when Kyle let me know immediately that he was in charge of the meeting. He showed me an image of himself sitting at a desk and a big smile on his face. I mentally thanked him for being there.

The meeting went well with information being given to the ladies about their children. One of Judy's friends had a son murdered, and it was very difficult for her to accept as it would be for any mother. I remember very clearly one of the words her son kept coming through with and that was "spaghetti." At first, it made no sense to her as she said she didn't cook. I felt ridiculous and wondered why the boys would put me through this ordeal. I kept mentally asking them to give me something else. Something that would ring a bell for this lady. But they would not. Her son would not give up though and kept making me repeat the word "spaghetti." After some time, she did acknowledge that she had made spaghetti just the week before. It was one of the few times she had cooked that week, and he was acknowledging it. I was thankful that she accepted that but it didn't make me feel any better. Spaghetti was too general. Many people cook spaghetti for dinner, so I wasn't pleased with his choice of confirmations. I asked him for something else a bit more specific. He then showed me a television game show. I told her about it and she said she did not watch game shows. Her son was persistent so I kept repeating that she had watched a game show that week and something particular on it had gotten her attention. The lady drew a blank.

Judy then spoke up and reminded her friend that she had indeed watched *Who Wants to be a Millionaire?* and one of the answers was a nickname that her son had been called.

She called Judy to tell her about it and she had wondered if it were a message from her son. I thanked Judy and Kyle for bringing it to light and helping me to learn to trust what I heard. The children are persistent in repeating their messages even though it must become frustrating to them at times.

Out of the blue during the meeting, this young man told me to talk about Allison. Judy acknowledged knowing someone who had lost a daughter named Allison, but that was all that was mentioned about her that night. It was a year later before that piece of the puzzle was connected.

Later during the evening, a different young spirit needed help coming through. He was shy and appeared to be embarrassed. I could mentally see Kyle pulling this young man through as if he were holding onto a rope. They were showing me the difficulty that it took to bring him in. This young soul had committed suicide, and it was hard for him to voice his feelings. Kyle helped with the information that the young spirit's mother acknowledged to be correct. That was the moment I learned the difference in energy levels and that not all spirits have the incredible energy that Kyle displays while he's around. I never knew Kyle in the physical world, but from what I understood from others, he was vibrant and made an impact on whomever he met. He brought that energy over with him, and I feel it whenever he is near.

After the meeting was over, I thanked Judy for allowing me to relay the messages from the children and later when I left, I saw a spider on my car door as I reached for the handle. I laughed to myself and also thanked Edgar. It had been an exciting night for me and I knew that this was the beginning of our project together.

I asked Kyle why he found it necessary to lead me to help the children on the Other Side. Here was his reply:

Simple. You have children of your own. You are in similar positions on a routine basis that allows us to provide you with the insight that can help others. You did not have just a girl. You also had two sons. What does that matter? All of your children are completely different in behavior in which allows us to give you many examples of the different types of parents and what they have experienced.

You have spent your entire life studying your children and their behavior, thought patterns, likes and dislikes. You have been a stay at home mother for that reason. You analyze what is needed for your children and you find unique ways to provide what is good for them. However you are not a perfect parent, because no one is, so this leaves us room to teach you lessons for your own growth. It is a package deal. We teach you and you share what you have learned.

Who is better able to teach than someone who is able to understand?

Chapter Eight

Turning Over New Pieces

After the meeting at Judy's house, I knew I needed to reach more people for more children. It was an urgency that wouldn't let me alone. I suppose it was Kyle and Edgar's working together for the children. They knew what was needed so they kept pushing me out of my shell, further and further, a little at a time.

I contacted a gentleman who had offered me the use of his building for other types of meetings and asked if he would allow me to hold a group meeting similar to what I had held at Judy's house. He was more than kind and agreed to help in any way he could. When I went to visit him at his office, two young men came through from the Other Side. I wasn't prepared to do a reading but I kept hearing them and saw the images they were showing me. I didn't think he had lost any children, so I didn't know how to approach him with what I was being shown. Finally, I asked him if he knew of two young men who had passed. He nodded that he did. I told him one of them was showing me a hotdog, and sandwich meats. He smiled and said, "They had a dachshund named Oscar."

I was shown that the boys were brothers and they were only interested in letting their mother know they were okay. I relayed that to him and he said he would pass that information onto his sister. The boys were his nephews. We then made arrangements for the meeting and I left.

I typed up flyers and mailed them out to anyone and everyone I knew who might be interested in coming to the meeting. Judy called all of the ladies she knew who had lost children and told them about it. The first meeting was scheduled on May 12th, but I kept having the feeling that no one would show up. I kept hearing the boys say, "Wait. It's still not time. Trust." I did wait and I did trust and only two people signed up. I decided to reschedule the meeting for a few weeks later and allow more people to sign up.

On the 25th of May, the meeting was held. Six people other than myself attended. Judy was excited for me. I will always remember her inspiring words. "Look, if you help just one person, it will be worth it!"

That phrase has made an imprint in my mind and will forever be there to remind me that everything has a reason, a purpose and a place.

During the meeting, I gave several people information they acknowledged to be true about their son or daughter. I tried to go in order of the way the people were seated, but when I came to one particular lady, I said, "I'm getting the name Lisa." She shook her head and said she didn't know of anyone by that name. Then I mentioned a letter.

The lady shook her head again and said it didn't apply to her. I was confused. I knew what I was hearing and seeing and she was not acknowledging it. So I sat there a moment and wondered what was going on. Finally, I asked again. "Are you sure that the name Lisa doesn't apply? I keep hearing that specific name very clearly."

She shrugged and said, "Not that I can think of."

Judy waved her hand at me and tried to get my attention. I looked her way and she said, "Can I interrupt a minute?"

I said, "Sure."

"I think Kyle is coming through," she said then smiled. "I got an e-mail from a lady named Lisa who wanted to attend, but she couldn't make it since she lives in Thibodaux. I brought the e-mail with me to tell you about it tonight because she wanted to know if you would go there and hold a meeting."

Then it seemed to make sense. Kyle was making sure that Judy gave me the message about Lisa. He already knew what the completed puzzle was going to look like, and tonight he was giving me a piece in a different section.

The rest of the meeting went well with many children coming through for their mothers. Even one lady who had come to hear from her sister who had just passed away ended up hearing from her son instead. Her son had been on the Other Side for many years and even though she knew he was okay, he still wanted to let her know he was around. The children don't give up when they want to be heard and for that I am thankful.

I asked Jason why we don't have control over who comes through and when. Here was his reply:

Because you are answering the phone, not dialing the number. Your process is more of the two-way radio. You ask if anyone is there and whoever is able to come through at that time will.

We send the messages as we feel they are needed. An example: suppose you send your child to the store to get a loaf of bread and you are also aware that someone you know works there that you need to send a message to. You will tell that message to your child and ask him to tell that person. It is that simple. Even though that person may have had no idea that you needed to get a message to them, you still took the opportunity to send it.

Many times families who come to hear from their children are not actually as 'ready' as they think. They haven't yet reached the point of surrendering them back to God. So instead, their message will come from another relative to ease the ear. Once that message is perceived and understood in the manner that it is implied, then the parent is ready to hear from their child.

Chapter Nine

Discovering a Different Part of the Picture

A short time after the meeting, I e-mailed Lisa and told her I would be happy to go to Thibodaux and hold a group meeting. She was excited that I agreed, and for several days afterwards we got acquainted through e-mail. I told her how I worked concerning the meetings, and she asked how I learned to do what I do and when I first realized I had this gift.

I recalled to her the night my father was killed in the car accident. My parents and sister were going to North Carolina for Thanksgiving. That day I stopped by to tell them goodbye. Just as I was leaving, I went to kiss my father goodbye, and he said, "If I don't see you again, take care of yourself and I love you." I was very touched by that because my father didn't express his sentiments very often. Even though I knew he loved me, he rarely said it. But I was also worried because it appeared that he thought there was a possibility that he might never see me again. My father had always been gifted with foresight. I had inherited it from him. However, he never talked about it. It was just understood between us.

That night I had been watching television and skimming through a book when I got a sharp pain on the right side of my head. It hurt so badly that I winced and grabbed my head. I immediately checked the clock and it was 9:50 p.m. I had learned from previous premonitions to check the clock and remember the time because it usually coincided with something occurring that I would learn about later.

My head was hurting so badly I had to go to bed. My eyes were blurry and I felt nauseous. Several hours later I got a call from Atlanta. My family had been hit from behind on the interstate and my father was in critical condition. The car had been hit at 10:50 eastern time, and my father had an

73

impact to the right side of his head. His brain stem was damaged, and they didn't think he was going to make it.

On Thanksgiving, after my family had returned to Baton Rouge and my father flown to Baton Rouge General, I realized he was going to die. My brother hadn't been able to fly to Atlanta, so I knew my father was just waiting until my brother could tell him goodbye before he crossed over. I had already said my goodbyes to him and knew it was a matter of time. I didn't stay with him. I knew he wouldn't have wanted that. Later that night after I had gotten my children to sleep and returned to our family room, I sat down beside my husband and cried.

At ten minutes till nine I suddenly felt different. I stopped crying and had such an exhilarating feeling. It was as if I were coasting down a hill on a bicycle with the wind hitting my face, and I couldn't catch my breath. It felt incredible! I turned to my husband and said, "Daddy just died. I felt it."

He looked at me strangely, but he could tell that something about me was different. I was no longer sad. I was overwhelmed with relief and excitement. I felt like there was a celebration going on, and I knew that my father was happy! It was almost like the excitement one feels when moving to a new home in a new state. First, there is the sadness of leaving friends and family behind, but the moment the destination is reached, the excitement of what lies beyond is exhilarating!

Ten minutes later, my mother called and told me that my father had indeed died and at the exact time I had first felt the strange but wonderful feeling of relief.

When I shared the story with Lisa, she seemed to understand in a way that brought us closer together as friends. I felt as if I had known her for a long time and felt comfortable sharing stories with her. As the days passed and she invited people to attend the meeting, she frequently asked me questions they had asked her. One question was whether or not we could tape record the meeting. I told her to feel free to do so, but I had learned through past experiences that tape recorders tend to malfunction during the sessions. I wasn't ever sure why, but it did happen on occasion.

We communicated by e-mail for a few weeks. Then the Saturday before Father's Day, just as I was getting ready to sign off, I heard a young man say, "Tell Mom to tell Dad not to forget the rake and garden tools tomorrow." I didn't recognize this person so I assumed it was Lisa's son, Jason, who had been killed in a motorcycle accident.

I debated whether or not to send that information along with the message I had just typed to her. I have always been leery of sharing unsolicited messages, but since Lisa had appeared to be open to after-death communication and had expressed genuine interest in what I was doing, I felt I had to share it with her. So I added a P.S. to the message and sent it on, wondering if it were Jason's way of sending a Father's Day message to his Dad.

Later that day she wrote back to me and told me upon first reading of my message, it didn't mean anything to her. But just out of curiosity, she called her husband, Terry, at the angel shop to see if it meant anything to him. She said there was a long pause on his end of the phone. Then he asked her how she knew he had just been talking with their neighbor at the shop about cleaning and fixing up the garden tomorrow morning? She explained to him about my P.S. message.

That was the day that Kyle introduced me to Jason.

Jason came to me with several other messages for his mother and father that I relayed by e-mail. He told me the words "pop" and "hoppy toad." I had no idea how they applied and neither did they. Lisa said Terry did have a diet soda with him but they have never referred to soft drinks as "pop." She also said he saw a green frog while cleaning the garden but wasn't sure that Jason would refer to it as a "hoppy toad." I told her not to make it fit but to let it present itself. I had learned to trust Kyle. Now I was learning to trust Jason.

Several days later, Lisa e-mailed me, once again so excited that her son's messages were making sense. Terry is a biologist and he hadn't been able to get toads for a couple of months, but the following Monday, after Jason's message, Terry's lab received an unexpected shipment of 600 toads. He called Lisa to share it with her.

Later we discovered that "pop" was actually the nickname of the man who previously owned the angel shop and had created the garden Terry had decided to clean.

I was thankful to Jason for allowing me to bring his parents comfort, but even more so the opportunity to show them how I communicated with the children so they could share this knowledge with others in need. The group meeting was set up in Thibodaux to be held on June 26th. I was excited and nervous about just what would happen that day.

I asked Edgar if the children knew when they were going to cross over to the Other Side. Here was his reply:

The children of your world know when they have accomplished what they have come to do. They give indications of such to their parents before their scheduled departure. Certainly it is a sad part of their journey but it is still a part that they must endure. Picture a child going away for summer camp. Tears flow of sadness and joy. But when the summer is over, they know they will once again be reunited. But going to summer camp is also prepared for. As the bags are packed, the rules are discussed for the behavior that is expected and then there is also the comforting that they will be there if they need them.

And when a child comes to our side, it is in reversal. The child prepares the parent with signs and messages that they wouldn't have normally expressed. The child goes with the hopes that the parent will be able to behave in an appropriate manner after they have gone and they show the parent that they indeed will always be with them. It is the same. An agreement. Both know that when the camp is over, they will reunite.

Sometimes a child in summer camp gets lonely and homesick. Sometimes a parent who loses a child gets lonely and wants their child to come back. As a parent, it is difficult to know that the child is sad and wants to come home from summer camp. As a child on the Other Side, it is difficult when a parent is sad and wants their child to come back. Not that the child doesn't sympathize with the parent, because they do. But it is just the same as the parent with a child at summer camp. The parent knows the child will be okay once he realizes this is where he is supposed to be for now.

Chapter Ten

Connecting the Odd Shaped Pieces

The following week, Heather and I were sitting in my computer room talking about our upcoming vacation. We had planned to go to Myrtle Beach in July and were really looking forward to it. We talked about the upcoming events and what we had hoped to do while in South Carolina.

Suddenly, I felt that I needed to listen to one of my old CDs. So I told Heather that I would be right back. I went back into the bedroom and randomly picked a CD I had bought several years before. It was a CD that had the hits from the early '60s. I brought it into the room where we had been talking and put it in the player.

Heather gave me a funny look. "What are you doing?"

"I don't know. I just have the feeling we're supposed to listen to this."

The first song was "Shop Around" by Smokey Robinson. The next thing I knew, Heather and I were trying to do the dances that were popular back in that time.

We laughed and giggled as we did the Mashed Potatoes, the Jerk, and the Swim to the music. We listened to several songs by Smokey Robinson and danced for about an hour. Neither of us knew what had come over us, but we had a great time just being silly, dancing and keeping to the beat of the music.

It didn't make sense to us why we were suddenly drawn to that music nor did we care. It was fun and we were enjoying ourselves. We danced until we were exhausted and just chalked it up to one of those weird unexplainable things.

The next day, on Friday June 23rd, Heather and I were sitting again in my computer room when I was alerted that an e-mail message had come in. I checked the address and noticed that it was not addressed to me but to someone I knew. I had accidentally received a message from Sue

Turner, a friend of a friend in Abilene, Texas. The message was originally addressed to Martha, but I somehow received it instead. At the time, I just thought it was e-mail malfunctioning and disregarded it as anything important.

But later after writing to Martha about it, I got an image of a man with a strong R in his name. So I questioned Martha if her friend Sue happened to know someone with a strong R who was on the Other Side. Martha wrote back and told me that Sue's son, Russ, had died less than a year before and that it was probably he. I then asked Martha if Sue would be open to spiritual communication with her son. She told me that Russ had been coming through several psychics with "messages for Mom." So she sent Sue my e-mail address and told her to contact me.

After several e-mail exchanges, I sent Sue messages from Russ. So many things made sense and explained the recent happenings and urges in my life, including my current desire to listen to 60's music. Sue informed me that she had just published a book about her son, Russell Knight Turner, called *Wings Born Out of Dust*. It tells the story of her son who was the youngest piano man for Frank Sinatra and later the musical director of Smokey Robinson's band for two and a half years.

When I read that, I knew Russ was the one who wanted me to listen to that music. It was his influence that led me to get the old CD and want to listen to Smokey Robinson.

Since I am open to their communication, I am easily swayed to enjoy what they want me to. Sometimes it is days or weeks before I learn who is influencing me with what. It is also very confusing understanding whether it is actually my own desire or something they are using to get my attention.

During my e-mails with Sue, I learned we had many similarities. For one, we both had sons named Russ. That wasn't so strange, but it was a coincidence. Second, her son had been playing music since he was twelve but didn't read music. Michael, my oldest son, has been playing music since he was 12 years old and also doesn't play by reading music. Both of them enjoy blues and jazz music more than any other kind. Russ played the piano and keyboard. Michael had just recently bought a keyboard and had decided to play it after almost ten years of playing the guitar. We couldn't understand the change at the time. That night before going to bed I wrote to her and commented to her that I found it to be more than coincidental.

The next morning after I woke up, I began sneezing. It was as if I had an allergy to something but I didn't know what. I wasn't normally a sneezer when I was allergic to something. I usually react with a headache or itching. So I couldn't understand what was bringing on the sneezing. I was miserable for hours. Since all I could manage to do was lie down, I began reading a book that I was comparing to Judy's book. It was a similar story but written in a different style. In that book, I read the lady called coincidences "synchronicity." I had never heard the word before and found it to be an interesting thought.

The dictionary states that coincidence is a remarkable occurrence of similar or corresponding events at the same time by chance. Synchronize means to cause to occur or operate at the same time. When I questioned the children about synchronicity, they showed me this analogy: a surprise birthday party. In this event, everyone plays a part. Usually someone has to call the folks together secretly setting up the time, date and location of where to meet. Someone else has to make sure the birthday person arrives at just the right moment and not too early to ruin what is supposed to happen. Then someone else stays at the appointed place to make sure all are ready to say "surprise" in unison so that the point of the party is that it takes on its desired form.

With that analogy understood, I realized that Sue's message coming to me was indeed synchronized.

A short while later, Sue answered my e-mail concerning coincidences and said she called it "synchronicity." That was the exact thing that I had just read less than an hour before! That was synchronicity in itself!

I knew there was a reason, so I tried to understand why all this synchronicity was happening within a few days. I sat staring at her message and sneezed. The children on the Other Side were trying to get attention, but I just couldn't figure it out.

I put it in order in my mind. Russ had influenced me enough to play the music. Then when his mother's e-mail came to me by mistake, I realized that it wasn't a mistake after all. Everything happens for a reason. So why was I sneezing and what were they trying to tell me? What was I reacting to?

I scanned through the other messages that I had received during the week, and then Lisa's message caught my attention. That was it! She had asked me if there were anything special she needed to do at the angel shop before I arrived and I said no. But there was something. I am highly allergic to potpourri and incense. I will get an extreme headache if I am near either one even for a short period of time. A bad headache would be the one thing that would prevent me from doing readings.

I quickly e-mailed Lisa and asked her if she could remove the potpourri and incense, if her store carried it, before I arrived and explained to her about my allergy to it. Once the message was sent, the allergy released and I didn't sneeze again.

Russ and Jason had joined forces and guided me to protect myself before the meeting. I had forgotten and would have been unable to give messages if I arrived and got an immediate headache. Russ and Jason knew what the completed picture was supposed to look like, and they were making sure that I didn't forget a few of the pieces and prevent it from connecting in its predestined form. That was the week that Jason introduced me to Russ.

Later, Sue sent me a copy of her book so I could get a closer insight to the new visitor who had joined my group. Russ' story is a sad but enlightening story of how someone so talented can end up homeless. Russ had much to show me in the form of communication. But soon he began to teach me that things aren't always what they seem.

I asked Russ how he was able to influence me enough to want to listen to '60s music. Here was his reply:

Let me whisper to you the thoughts of another and see if they don't appear to be yours after a while.

You see, when a thought is mentioned aloud it becomes more than just a thought, but an energy form. And that energy form takes hold of the emotions of the people that are near. For example, if you were to go to a movie and smell the buttery scent of popcorn, you would soon feel as if you wanted that even though you may not be hungry. Another example is when a person sits in a room with someone who is gloomy. If the thoughts are expressed enough, the gloom becomes a reality and all who enter the room begin to feel it. However if you enter a room of laughter and cheer, you too, will begin to feel cheerful. Have you ever walked into a room when there was tension among the people? Of course, hence the phrase 'you could cut the tension with a knife.'

But, the example that answers your question is this, suppose you began to hear music that was pleasing to the ear but not actually your preference. In time you would decide that you wanted to listen to more. The music itself leaves an energy form in which can recreate itself in the existence of the realm of energy that permeates the body...hence the phrase 'he has rhythm.'

So as spirits trying to convey a message to our loved ones, we create the thought form and send it out to you so that you may respond in a positive manner.

Chapter Eleven

Discovering the Theme of the Puzzle

Monday morning, on June 26th, Judy and I headed out for Thibodaux. Both of us were nervous and excited. Judy had printed out a map from the Internet on how to get there so we followed its directions, laughing and talking all the way. I had been to Thibodaux only once before, and it bothered me having to drive across the Sunshine Bridge. I dreaded that bridge and it made me nervous to even think about it, but as she followed the directions, I discovered that a new bridge had been completed in Gramercy in which was not quite as high as the Sunshine Bridge. It didn't bother me riding across it. As a matter of fact, it was very picturesque. The Mississippi River was calm with barges moving slowly through it at a distance. The land on both sides of the river was green and flourishing.

We arrived early and stopped at the Holiday Inn in Thibodaux to eat lunch. I was too nervous to eat much. I ate a baked potato and a piece of lemon pie.

The meeting was scheduled for 1:00 so we arrived at Bryson's Angel Shop around 12:30.

Lisa introduced herself and welcomed me with a hug. Being raised in the north by parents who were not accustomed to showing their affections, I was surprised by Lisa's gesture. But I returned the hug and immediately sensed that we would become longtime friends.

As she spoke about her excitement concerning the meeting, I noticed her voice had an unusually soothing tone. There was a calm and peaceful quality to it that contradicted her e-mail messages. Her messages had been written with many exclamation points and descriptive words. Yet her voice was so calming that I instantly felt relaxed, and my apprehensions vanished. I knew that the children on the Other Side had led me to the right place.

The shop was decorated with an assortment of angels and greenery. Lisa showed me she had moved the potpourri into a different room. I mentally thanked the kids for reminding me, knowing that I would have suffered greatly had they not done so. I was happy to be there. The place felt so comfortable, so right. There was such a welcoming atmosphere, yet there was something I couldn't put my finger on. I was still looking for signs that the children on the Other Side were with me. I hadn't seen any spiders or gnats, and there were no signs of animals. I was wondering if the boys had gotten me there and abandoned me.

At 1:00, eleven people had arrived for the meeting. Lisa arranged the chairs in a circle, and I sat in one of them closest to the window. Lisa sat beside me and set up the tape recorder and the microphone so we could tape the session.

I introduced myself and gave a brief description of what I was going to do, which I find the most difficult part of my job. I have never been good at public speaking and the thought of talking about myself embarrassed me. I mainly wanted just to help the people. I found it unnecessary to talk about myself.

Since Lisa was sitting to my left, I began with her. I gave her information that she wrote down, smiling all the while. I learned that she was my gauge on whether or not I was supplying a significant piece of information. So many times her eyebrows would lift or she would just shake her head in disbelief because I had touched on many things that were going on in her life. She was a wonderful first person to read for because she acknowledged what I was telling her as truth.

After all, I had eleven people facing me that were counting on me to give them messages from their children, and I didn't want to let them down.

After Jason came through with much information for his mother, I was able to move on to the others with confidence knowing at least some of the children had shown up. Lisa knew several of the people whom I read for, so when I gave them accurate information I could always tell by the look on her face. Her eyes would light up and her smile would widen, acknowledging the truth in what I had relayed to them. The ladies whom I read for were so speechless at what I was telling them that most could barely nod their heads in acknowledgment. It was only when their eyes became moist with tears that I knew they understood what I was telling them. But I was still very thankful that Lisa was gauging my work at that point.

After giving readings to several other mothers, however, Russ showed up to remind me that things aren't always what they seem. When the next reading began, I told the mother that I was getting an image of a young child.

She nodded in acknowledgment.

This child showed me a very short haircut.

"I am also being shown a baseball," I told her.

I could see the stunned look in her eyes, the look that tells me I have touched on something significant. "I am being shown a bucket of Legos."

The young mother's mouth dropped open and she slowly nodded, still not saying anything, but her eyes showed a hint of recognition.

As soon as I was shown a strong E, R, and N in the name, I guessed the name Ernie. I had automatically assumed that because of the short haircut and boys' toys, this child was a male.

She shook her head. "No, my daughter's name was Erin."

Later she explained that her daughter kept her hair cut very, very short and she carried a bucket of Legos around with her everywhere. The significance of the baseball was that Erin died during the last tournament of the season. Her father was a coach for the team and found it too difficult to continue. Even though the team had been in the loser's bracket, the team ended up taking first place in the tournament. Erin had brought through what she thought was the most important information to her and her family.

I realized then that I could no longer assume anything from the spirit world and that by stereotyping, I would be misleading myself and others.

Russ didn't stop there. Toward the end of the meeting, I read for a lady whose child came across very shyly. Jason gave me a mental image of literally pulling this teen into my vision so that I could give a reading. I was then given the image of long blond hair and even though I had just been previously warned not to stereotype, my nature automatically made me assume that long hair was a girl. So I told the mom that a teenager girl was coming through with long blond hair. The lady shook her head no.

The child knew I was going off track, so I felt the sensation that my lungs had been crushed and I was shown a car accident.

When I told her that, she nodded.

"Jason is showing me that he went to school with your child. Is that correct?" I asked her.

She nodded slowly.

"Does your child have blond hair?" I asked.

"Yes," she began. "But it wasn't long."

"Is your child on the Other Side a girl?"

"No," she replied.

I couldn't understand it. I was being shown this very long blond hair and the energy I felt from this spirit was so gentle, I thought maybe I was picking up on the wrong child for her.

"Now wait, let's figure this out," I said in an attempt to put together the pieces of what we had been shown so far. "Your child did go to school with Jason. Your child was in a car accident. But your child had short blond hair. Is that correct?" I asked.

She nodded.

"Then why am I getting very long blond hair?" I was confused.

She shrugged then said, "Well, Clint always wanted to grow it long."

As soon as she said that, I heard her son laugh. He told me to tell her that it was long now. I smiled at what I was hearing from him. I looked around and noticed all were watching. I tend to forget sometimes that I am being watched because I am so busy listening to the Other Side.

It is like relaying a phone call to someone while they are in the room. I listen a moment to what is being said, then I repeat it to the person facing me. If you have ever relayed a phone call like that, then you know how hard it is to concentrate on both people at once. Some words can get lost in translation.

"He just told me to tell you that he has it long now," I told them.

Everyone in the room began laughing.

I learned later that after Clint's accident, his brother had dreamed of his having long hair and Clint had indicated to him that he was able to accomplish things over there he couldn't do while here. On a separate occasion, a friend of Clint's went to his mother and told her of a dream he had about Clint and his hair was long then, also.

That day the children had gathered to teach me several things. I knew Edgar and Kyle were teaching me always to trust that they would bring the children through.

Erin taught me not to stereotype and Clint taught me that children are able to do things they've always wanted to once they reach the Other Side. Russ taught me that not everything is as it seems and Jason taught me that they all work together to synchronize the events.

I asked Russ why he came to help people who were dealing with addictions. Here was his reply:

When a parent loses a child, there is a hole that can't seem to be filled. The parent feels the loss like no other. The hole is empty and stays that way until the parent and child reunite in the afterlife.

Physical beings depend on nurturing in their existence. They look for something to fill that void. Sometimes parents turn to alcohol or drugs to fill that empty spot that they can't seem to fill any other way. It is not a choice they make, it is a need they feel they have to fill.

Though after time passes and the parent realizes that nothing fills that void that can be found in the physical, they have weakened their body to the point of having to work again from the ground up. It is devastating and sometimes the road is much longer and harder than expected. Once the parent discovers that the only thing that can fill that void is the promise of the afterlife, they begin to heal. They begin to know that God has indeed kept his promise that we will reunite again. That death was not the end but merely a different type of journey. The road changed midway and now both participants have to make their own discoveries before meeting again.

Parents who choose the addiction to fill the void have not yet found what is needed to acquaint their spirit with their soul. They rely on physical sources to provide the nurturing that their loneliness takes from them. In order to help the parent become more aware of their need to be nurtured, the child must find a way to communicate with them. The child tries desperately to help their parents see that they are now in God's hands. The grieving parent sometimes questions how God could have taken their child from them and questions if possibly they weren't doing a good enough job in the physical.

There is no basis for that thought except the loss of faith. When a parent has lost faith in the higher energy source, they have lost faith in themselves.

In answer to your question, it is needed for parents not to be given drugs or alcohol to ease the grieving process. It is needed to give the parents proof that their child is doing well in the afterlife and the reuniting will occur as promised.

Chapter Twelve

Finding Pieces That Have Been Hidden

Weeks later, Heather and I took the trip to Myrtle Beach. It was a girls' vacation and one we felt we really needed at the time. We had asked the spirit world not to accompany us on this trip nor give us any symbols or signs that needed to be figured out. We normally found the symbolism to be exciting and each spirit presented a new learning experience. But this trip was supposed to be fun, and we just wanted a break from it for a week.

The vacation turned out to be quite enjoyable, and we dismissed any possibility of a sign as a coincidence just for the sake of rest and relaxation. We had literally turned off our phones to the spiritual world and we weren't even taking messages.

However, we didn't realize at the time that we had a call forwarded to our home. We discovered it one Saturday morning.

We had been back from our vacation for several weeks and I hadn't taken the time yet to go through the piles of memorabilia that we had gathered on the trip. That Saturday morning I found a newspaper I had picked up in a small town outside of Birmingham. Heather and I had spent the night there in an effort to break up the long trip back home.

I was going to toss the paper into the trash when I kept feeling like there was something in it that I needed to see. I was sitting in my computer room drinking coffee and everyone else was asleep. I stared at the folded paper and kept hearing "look inside." I opened it up, turned the pages and saw a picture of a young girl who had been murdered. Her name was Emily, and she was an art student in the town where we had stopped. The picture was printed as an "in loving memory" type of article. I looked at her innocent face with long dark brown hair. Her eyes seemed to beckon me.

The picture showed her standing beside a portrait that she had painted of a ballerina. My heart went out to her and her family.

I wasn't sure why I had been drawn to look at the picture. Maybe someone new was coming to our home. It had been weeks since Heather and I returned, and we hadn't seen any particular signs or symbols. We had begun to think that maybe we had scared the spirits off completely. We even joked about making them mad or evicting them, but then we began to notice an anger between the two of us that hadn't been there before. At first I just thought it was the let down after the vacation. Later, I assumed it was a phase that we were going through. A mother/daughter phase. So I hadn't been overly concerned about it. I figured it would pass in time.

I folded up the newspaper and put it aside. Suddenly, I heard footsteps in the kitchen. I looked up to see Heather, sleepy eyed, coming into my room. She plopped down on the floor and turned to face me. "I had a very weird dream last night! It scared me. Do you want to hear it?"

"Of course," I said, knowing she would tell me anyway. We always discussed our dreams. It gave us insight into what we would be dealing with in the future. Sometimes it showed us what we were dealing with in the present that we had possibly overlooked in our hurried lifestyle.

"I dreamed," she began, rubbing her eyes, "that a young girl was sitting at the bottom of our driveway painting a picture."

I began to get the traces of goose bumps. "Really?"

"Yes. But she was not happy. She was really upset. And in the dream, I remember going out to a big field. In that field was a knife. It had been there for a long time because the grass under it was yellow."

I sat there knowing who our next visitor was. Emily. But I didn't offer any information. I waited, listening for more confirmations.

"I knew we were in another town, though, because it didn't look familiar. It was like we had moved and our driveway was somewhere else." She rubbed her eyes again and yawned. "I don't know who the girl was. I don't think I have ever seen her before."

I reached over and pulled out the newspaper. I opened it up to the page where Emily's picture was printed, then handed it to Heather.

Heather raised her eyebrows. "Wow. This looks like her." She glanced at the paper. "We bought this paper when we were on vacation, didn't we?"

I nodded. "Guess who followed us home?"

"When did you see that article?" she asked.

"Just a minute before you walked in, why?"

"Do you think I picked up on it in my sleep?" she questioned, never allowing coincidence to play a part in our piecing together the puzzle.

"No. That would be impossible," I assured her.

Heather had been known to pick up on what I had read or typed during her sleep. Many times I would receive an e-mail from a friend early in the morning, during the time when she was still sleeping in bed, and she would get up and recite a dream that had the basic concept of what was in the e-mail message. At first we thought it was coincidental. Then we learned there was no such thing.

"Why impossible?" she asked.

"Because I just read it moments before you came walking into my room. Unless you were sleep walking, it couldn't have happened."

She laughed. Then her face became serious. "So why do you think she is here?"

"The usual reason, I guess. She wants to contact her parents."

Heather reached for the newspaper and scanned the article. "It says her murderer was never found."

Fear shivered through me. I didn't want to consider trying to find the murderer. I don't mind helping anyone, but I didn't want to get involved in something like that. I knew very little about police procedures at the time, and I didn't want to step in where I didn't belong.

"So what do we do now?" Heather asked.

"Just let her give us the signs, I guess, and see where we go from there."

A few weeks passed and we didn't seem to notice anything new. School had begun, and Heather had gotten a bit more irritable than usual. I thought it was the stress of beginning high school, but then I found myself to be on edge quite a bit, getting angry at the smallest things. It was such a change from the summer when we had been so silly and enjoyed music and our new visitors. Learning the signs and symbols had been a challenge we often enjoyed. But Heather began to complain that it was no longer fun and she wanted them to leave her alone. I found myself getting irritated at the constant feeling of tension that now inhabited our home, yet it was only between Heather and me. We were easily angered, and it just wasn't like us to be that way. We were chewing everyone's head off who got in our path.

About two weeks later, I dreamed about Emily. She was holding my hand and taking me to a place that was melancholy. I wandered around in this place and felt sadness that was so overwhelming I couldn't release it. It was terrible. I asked her to take me back, but she wouldn't unless I agreed to help her. The grief that I was feeling was unlike anything I had ever experienced. I knew she was trying to show me what it was like for her family, and she wanted to help them. When they were grieving so deeply, she too, was having a difficult time. She wanted to show them that she was indeed okay and that she needed their acceptance of that to move on. She was lodged in a place of sadness because she couldn't get them to let her go.

I woke up knowing I had to help her. That day I talked with Heather about it and told her we had to do something about contacting Emily's family. I just didn't know what. I had no idea whether her family would be open to spiritual communication, and I didn't want to cause them further grief.

For days I deliberated on what I should do and how I should handle the circumstances. I kept hearing, "Call Pat, she'll know." I had never heard Emily's voice before, yet I had also never had a female communicate with me that way, so I gathered it was she. So I called my good friend, Pat, and asked her to meet me for lunch. When she quickly agreed, I just had the feeling that Pat would know how to help. I wasn't sure why, but I knew she could. We had tried to meet for lunch on many occasions before but each time something out of our control had prevented it. So when she was able to meet, I knew a spiritual intervention had begun.

During lunch, I confided in Pat and shared the entire story about Emily. When I told her about the town outside of Birmingham where I had bought the newspaper, Pat's eyes lit up.

"I have a friend who lives there who worked for the police department. He is retired but he may be able to help."

I then heard Emily say, "See?" I smiled to myself.

"Do you think he would be open to this?" I asked Pat.

She nodded. "Yes. I do. He's a very spiritual person actually."

We spent the rest of our lunch discussing how we could handle this new case that had been presented to us.

A few days later, Pat called to give me the number of her friend. She told me that she had spoken with him and that he would be very interested in anything I could say to help the case.

I wasn't interested in helping with the case, though I would if I could. I was more interested in contacting her parents and helping them. Emily didn't come to me in a dream and show me the details of the crime and how I could help the police locate the criminal. That was not her concern. She was concerned about the state of mind of her grieving parents.

I took the number from Pat and called him. He was a pleasant man with a sincere interest in his voice as we spoke. I told him it was hard for me to discuss this sort of thing since I wasn't the one being sought after. He understood and

103

tried to make the call as easy as possible. I was unable to give him any information concerning the case, as I had expected. I did ask him to locate her parents and find out if they would be interested in my help otherwise. He said he would. I gave him my phone number and e-mail address and told him to have them contact me if they were interested.

They never did.

A month passed and I never heard from any of them. But during that time, Heather and I became more angry and frustrated, experiencing emotions that were very much out of character for us. We were having moods swings that scared even us.

One day when Heather had just finished slamming her books down, she looked up at me and said, "Mom, I think this is Emily."

I stopped for a moment and stared at her. "What do you mean?"

"Remember how when Russ came through we started dancing to the 60's songs?" she asked.

"Yes."

"Well, I have been seeing paintings of ballerinas everywhere. On television. In books at school. In movies. Everywhere. And I'm not looking for them. It is like they are finding me. And I know she is around. She is showing us how angry she is that we aren't helping."

She was right. That wise old spirit within my young daughter was correct once again, and I hadn't noticed it. Even though I live a good bit of my life connected to the spirit world, I am still a part of the physical world living out human emotions and experiencing insecurities and curiosities like everyone else. With the usual pressures of daily life, I had overlooked that we could be experiencing yet another one of the spiritual visitor's reactions. I had just believed that since her parents nor the detective ever called or e-mailed, it was over and not going to be carried any further. But Emily had other plans. She was expressing her anger through us and waiting until the right moment for us to take notice.

Thank goodness Heather finally did.

"So, what do we do now?" I asked my ancient wonder.

Heather sighed. "I don't know but we have to do something. I don't like feeling like this all the time."

"Well, we could go to the little town where we bought the newspaper and look around. Possibly go to her grave," I suggested, not really meaning to do so.

"That sounds like a good idea!" Heather was always up for new adventures, especially if it meant traveling. I am normally a homebody and it takes a dire need for clothing for me even to go shopping. Visiting a mall is usually a once-a-year thing. Thank goodness for catalogs.

"No. I was just kidding. I don't want to drive all the way there. Besides, what would we do when we arrived? I'll bet there are lots of cemeteries in that town. I don't want to go all the way there and spend days looking for a gravesite. Then what? We don't even know if her parents are receptive to this type of thing."

"Please, Mom. It's either that or we destroy the house in anger," she joked.

On second thought, I wanted to see our moods get back to normal, and I didn't think Emily was going to be leaving anytime soon.

"I'll talk to Dad and see what he thinks and let you know."

Heather smiled her knowing smile. I knew she was already mentally packing her things.

The following day I spoke aloud to Emily. "If you want us to go to your home town, then give me a sign that there should be a reason for me to go. Otherwise, I may not waste my time and money. And speaking of money, if you want us to go, get Kyle to lead my husband to the winning slot machine. I shouldn't have to pay for this trip."

That afternoon after I picked up Heather from school, an announcement came on the radio concerning an arts and crafts show. There were several of them scheduled from here to where else but the little town outside of Birmingham. Heather looked at me, surprise engulfing her face. "See,

Mom. Now we have a reason to go. We can look at arts and crafts."

I'm not an arts and crafts lover, but Heather is. She makes crafts and also appreciates others' work.

I knew that was Emily's sign, so I had to go with it. "Okay. We'll go," I said, though I wasn't too happy about it. Yet, it seemed good compared to my alternative.

Later that afternoon, my husband, Bob, called me from the casino boat. He had the urge to stop by on his way back from a meeting at work. He hadn't planned to go, but he said something led him there and he just felt as if he were going to win.

"So, want to go out to dinner?" he asked.

"Why, did you win?" I asked.

"Oh, yeah," he said with a hearty laugh.

I thanked Kyle mentally, then Emily, and at the same time wondered just what I was getting myself into later down the road.

I asked Tanya why the children come to me before the parent does. Here was her reply:

If you were in a foreign country and could not speak the language, would you perhaps find an interpreter? That is why we come to you. We know you will understand our language and therefore relay it in the manner that we express it.

If you were a teacher and watching your young students perform in class, whom would you choose to help the new student who arrives? The one most capable, of course. The student who is active in the class, who is aware of what is going on, being taught and constantly seeking to learn more. That is why we come to you. You have spent your entire life looking for answers, solving mysteries and questioning all there is to life.

You love a good mystery and we know that.

Chapter Thirteen

Putting Pieces in Unlikely Places

The weekend arrived for the arts and crafts show to be held. Heather and I got up early and left. We were going to just stay the day and drive back that evening. We didn't want to spend the night because we had plans for the following day.

The ride was enjoyable. The weather beautiful. We were accompanied by a gnat for the first part of the morning. Heather pointed it out once we had been on the road for about thirty minutes. "Well, we know Edgar is along."

I smiled, thinking to myself, "What have I done to this poor girl? She will never have a 'normal' lifestyle."

Later down the highway, we spotted a huge black crow sitting on the railing of a small bridge. It stayed in place as we passed by it. "Kyle's here, too," we said in unison and then laughed.

Hours later we reached the small town. We couldn't find the craft show at first, but we had expected that. A sense of direction was not our long suit. We usually had to be led wherever we were going. Finding things on our own, well, it just wasn't normal to us and maybe that was to our advantage. We were open to spiritual intervention to lead us to wherever we needed to be.

After many U-turns and backtrackings, we finally located the street where the arts and crafts show was held. It was an outdoor show and held on the sidewalk. Heather and I walked up and down the sidewalks enjoying the scenery, small talk and beautiful crisp autumn weather.

We stopped inside a small café and ate lunch. The day went by well, but I didn't feel as if we were accomplishing anything as far as Emily was concerned.

Afterwards, we located a cemetery and walked around a while reading all the names. We couldn't find Emily's name anywhere, and we weren't even sure if we were at the right cemetery. Heather and I walked up the many rows of headstones getting tired and ready to go home.

"Okay, Emily, if you want our help, you're going to have to put forth a little effort here," I said. "We've come this far."

Heather went ahead of me and looked at more gravestones. She returned after a few minutes. "I don't think this is it, Mom. I'm not receiving any signs at all. I felt like we were more on track at the craft show."

I knew she wanted to shop a little more, but I also trusted her intuition. She had been taught at an early age to go with her gut feeling and not to deny it. God had given it to us for a reason just like every other sense.

We got into the van and headed back to the crafts show. We parked in a different location this time and decided to walk in another direction. We found a little ice cream shop and went in to get something to drink. While there, Heather noticed that everything seemed to be doubled. Two chairs were arranged by themselves with no one in them. Two straws were lying on the floor beneath a table, and two pictures hanging on the wall were of ballerinas.

We bought our drinks and when we walked outside, she began pointing at the license plates. Several of the cars had plates that had double numbering or double lettering. I shrugged questioning.

"Don't you get it?" she asked. "Whatever Emily wants us to find is two something over. Either two streets or two buildings. See?"

I had begun to get tired and my deduction abilities were wavering. It did make sense, but it hadn't occurred to me. "Let's try the second building first. I'm getting tired of walking."

When we rounded the corner and walked two buildings down, there was an antique shop. Heather loves antiques so that got her attention immediately. We walked inside and began looking around. The shop had clothing from the 1800's. The elderly lady who sat behind the counter smiled

112

a wrinkled face and said, "Go ahead and try on a few if you want."

Heather pulled out the dresses and looked at them, smiling and frowning alternately. She picked up a big hat with a feather on it and placed it on her head.

I quickly pulled my camera from my purse and clicked a few pictures. We had gotten tired and silly, and it was beginning to get dark. So I suggested we begin our drive home. Heather was disappointed but agreed. Just as we went out the door, Heather gave a model-like pose in front of the door, and I clicked one more picture of her.

We found our way back to the van, disappointed and wondering what had been the point of this trip. It didn't make sense, and we found nothing that connected us with Emily.

Later that week after I had developed the pictures, I found the one of Heather standing in front of the antique shop to be particularly intriguing. She was making an unusual face in the picture, and it made me smile every time I saw it. So I pinned it up by my computer.

Each time I glanced at that picture I wondered why Emily wanted us to go to that antique shop. What was there that would have been significant for us to find?

A week passed and then one day I glanced at the picture and something in it caught my eye. The name of the shop was printed on the door and their phone number was underneath. Should I call the owner and possibly ask her if she knew Emily or her parents? It seemed to be a small town, and a murder like that probably would have been discussed for a good while. But it had been many years since the murder had occurred.

I dropped the idea and let it go. I knew I was stretching the limits. What if I did find her parents? What would I say then? Something like "Hey, your deceased daughter is at my home; would you like to talk to her?" No, it was too farfetched. I had to give up the idea for a while. It was getting the best of me.

The next day, I woke up knowing I had to call despite my earlier fears. There was no other choice. I called the lady at the shop and asked if she happened to know Emily.

She said she did. Emily's mother had been a good friend of her daughter's for years. Emily had even worked in the antique shop part time for a while. She also said that there was an address they had given to the police for anyone who might have information about the crime and asked if I wanted it. I said yes.

That day I wrote a long letter to Emily's mother. I explained what I did and what I had hoped to accomplish. It was a very difficult letter to write. I didn't want to scare her mother away. It had taken me months to get this far in Emily's quest. I sealed it, mailed it and told Emily the rest was up to her.

It was many months later before I was able to meet with her mother.

I asked Tanya why don't the children on the Other Side just tell us in plain language what they want us to know instead of giving us signs that lead us here and there. Here was her reply:

We give you the information that is needed at the moment. If you were a kindergarten teacher, would you tell your children to get their lunch boxes out two hours before lunchtime? Of course not. We work with many people at many times at once. It is because of that we must give what we can and what will suffice. Let me give you an example. Suppose you were teaching kindergarten children how to say their ABCs. Would you start with the letter 'K' and then work backward? Would you start with the letter 'F' and work forward? Of course not. You would begin with the letter 'A.' You would show them how that applies and what it relates to. You would give them images to put in their head that they could associate with the letter 'A' such as the word 'apple.' When that was formed and well understood, you would move onto the letter 'B' and do the same thing.

If you said, ABCDEFGHIJKLMNOPQRSTUVWXYZ in a matter of seconds, would you believe they would know how it all applied and what the purpose was? No, because you took away the learning of word association.

Too much too soon takes away from the experience of learning and that is what the spiritual world is all about.

Chapter Fourteen

Shapes That Connect Beautifully

In October, I went to a specialty store to buy a gift for Judy for her birthday. I had no idea what to buy but was led to that particular store. While there, I went to an aisle that had a display of framed pictures and artwork. I scanned through the many landscapes and flowered pictures, never quite finding anything that appealed to me nor what I thought Judy would like.

After about fifteen minutes I came across a small, framed picture of a starfish. It was very basic and not the type of gift I would relate to Judy, yet something about it made me want to get it for her. I kept hearing, "Mom will like it." I knew Kyle was trying to influence me and at that point it was okay, because as I said, I really didn't know what to buy. So after picking it up and putting it down about five times, I finally decided to buy it.

A few weeks later, Judy and I were on our way to Thibodaux for another group meeting. I gave her the gift and she was pleased. She said she and Kyle had found a huge starfish many years ago when they were together at the Puget Sound. Once more, it was comforting to know that the children were always accurate and precise with their insightful guidance. Later I learned how much it would be appreciated.

We reached Thibodaux and went in to visit with Lisa before the group arrived. Lisa had told me ahead of time that an unusual circumstance brought a couple into her store the previous week and they were now also included in this group. I asked her not to give me the details until after the meeting. I didn't want any knowledge of the couple that might interfere with what I was trying to interpret from the Other Side.

I had also asked her to ask the participants to bring something of the child's that I could hold in my hand while giving the reading. I thought maybe that would help connect me better with the children and prevent mixed messages from popping in.

When it was time to read for the couple, I read for the man first. I asked him his first name, and he said Dave.

"Others are bringing in a baby while grandfather Louis is coming through," I said.

Dave acknowledged that he had a grandfather named Louis.

"The baby says he is one of two names, his and one on this side with the name David in it."

Dave nodded yes. "My son's name is Scott. His son's name is Scotty. And Scotty's middle name is David."

Nettie, his wife, then spoke up and asked, "Could you tell me how this baby passed?"

I nodded. "Yes."

Nettie got up and handed me a piece of clothing that belonged to the baby.

I held the soft pajamas in my hands and immediately got an image of a baby getting strangled on its own saliva. "You know how it feels when saliva goes down the wrong pipe?" I touched my throat because I had suddenly felt a loss of breath, a feeling of suffocation. "Did this baby have a breathing problem?"

"Yes."

"He was having problems breathing, and when he went to swallow a saliva like liquid, he choked. He said he felt he was being strangled. He was coughing, congested and having a hard time breathing."

Nettie later told me that if she could have asked only one question, that would have been the one. The answer to that question was the main reason she and Dave had asked to attend the meeting.

Nettie acknowledged that Scotty was born with a breathing problem, spending ten days in the hospital on life support before he came home.

"Scotty said he was not meant to live a long time. It became dangerous and difficult," I told her. "He wants to acknowledge his nurse. Her name started with a J."

Nettie nodded. "His nurse's name was Jenny."

"He is also showing me that there is a young girl with the letters A and M in her name. He wants her to know that he felt her love coming through."

Nettie acknowledged that Scotty's godmother's name was Aimee Michele, and she took her job very seriously, loving him as if he were her own.

I could feel a shift in energy, and suddenly Scotty showed me something entirely different. "Someone in the family backed into a post, causing minor damages."

Dave nodded. "Yes, my son, Scott, did that last week."

I immediately felt a sharp pain to my head. "Scotty is showing me that his father suffers from migraine headaches due to stress."

Dave nodded.

"Scotty also shows me that his father will receive a promotion and never look back."

Nettie later told me that her son did receive the promotion.

Next, I felt pulled to look at only Nettie. I knew this information was directed mostly toward her, however, during Dave's reading it was meant for both of them as I could feel Scotty bouncing me back and forth to their questions and replies. I had never read for a couple who were so open and the information flowed as it did at that time. It was like turning on a switch and allowing the information to run through my mind like a ticker tape.

"Scotty shows me he will get older as you get older. He will not stay a baby on the Other Side," I told Nettie. "As his sister matures, he will be coming to her in her dreams and when this happens, believe what she is saying because it will be true."

"Lisa," Nettie said.

Nettie told me later that his three-year-old sister, Lisa, does see him now in spirit form and plays with him daily.

121

"Scotty says that Lisa has a doll and it wears a dress that belonged to Lisa. It is yellow."

Nettie told me later she had sent a message to Scotty before she went to the meeting. She held the doll in her hands and said, "This is a doll that is different from the rest. If this is real and I can trust what I am told, send this back to me. This doll is for Lisa and it wears one of her baby gowns. It is white with yellow flowers and pictures on it."

I continued, "When you smell a powdery scent in the house, it will be him."

Nettie acknowledged noticing the scent since he had passed.

The energy changed again, and I felt a shift. "Grandfather Louis is telling me you need to look at one of the last pictures taken. There is a blur in the corner of it. It is he. He wanted his picture taken."

Nettie told me later that she had taken a picture of Scotty during his christening. It was the second to last picture ever taken of him. There is a blur in the left corner. It looked like the image of someone. Grandfather Louis had only had one picture taken of him that the family knew of and it had been borrowed and never returned.

"Scotty is showing me a birth certificate. Do you know why he is showing me this?"

"His family's birth certificates were all lost in a move."

"Scotty tells me he was called a nickname. He was called Pudgy or something with this sound."

"Pudgy Wudgy face," she replied.

The information kept rolling in, and I was happy to oblige. "There is a horse-like stuffed animal. It is not a regular stuffed animal. It has a giraffe-life face. The mane on it is reddish brown and made of yarn along with its tail."

Nettie gave me a blank look and shrugged.

I was surprised because everything had made sense to her and Dave from the beginning. But I knew what I had seen and it was very clear.

After the meeting, Nettie went home and checked the closet where she kept the animals, and in the center was a horse with the exact color that had been described along with a giraffe-like face. It was different from a regular stuffed animal because it was a Beanie Baby horse.

"There will be a celebration in December other than Christmas. It would be on or around the 18th," I told her next.

Scotty's godmother graduated from college and Nettie attended her party on the 19th. She went to buy her some flowers and balloons and the only balloon that she could find that was appropriate was one that read "celebration" on it. When Nettie saw the balloon at the party, it dawned on her what Scotty had meant.

"The number four, six and the 18th has a special meaning," I said.

"Scotty was almost four months old when he passed. My birthday is on the 18th," she said.

I could feel the reading was coming to a close, but Scotty had one last message that he felt the need to share with his grandmother and grandfather. "He tells me he could be of more help to you on the Other Side than he could ever be here."

Almost a year later, Nettie told me what brought her to Bryson's Angels that day. She said Scotty had died in November and his death and the circumstances surrounding it had left her feeling unsettled. She questioned it daily, and it soon became an obsession for her to try and find the answer to her question.

One day she was led to Bryson's Angels. She walked around a while, yet wasn't sure why she was in there. After finding a picture of an angel in the clouds with a story about a grandmother who had lost a baby to SIDS written on the back of it, she assumed that was the reason. Since she still was not convinced, she spoke with Terry about it. He then shared a dream that he had about his son, Jason bringing a baby to him. He didn't know who the baby was and had only dreamt of Jason three times since his death six years before. After discussing this with Nettie, he guessed that perhaps Scotty was the baby that Jason had brought to him in the dream. Terry went on to explain that he and Lisa had been to New Orleans to see John Edward and told Nettie how remarkable he had been. Nettie had never heard of John Edward at the time and had no idea that such communication was possible.

Eleven months passed and Nettie still felt unsettled. Her beliefs conflicted with what the hospital had told her. Then the Saturday before my group reading, Nettie and Dave went for a ride and once again ended up at Bryson's Angels. After shopping and visiting with Lisa and Terry, Nettie suddenly found herself asking, "Do you know when the man is coming back that you and Terry went to see in New Orleans?"

Lisa asked, "Why?"

"Because I need an answer to my question," Nettie replied.

Lisa told her to sit down.

Nettie asked, "Why? Are you going to tell me this will pass?"

"No," Lisa replied softly.

Nettie gave her a questioning look.

"I have someone coming here that might can help you."

Lisa had left two spaces open for the meeting and hadn't a clue why at the time. Evidently Jason and Scotty had known all along.

I had asked Jason why babies came into our lives for only a brief period of time and then crossed over. This time Tanya stepped in. Here was her reply:

In a matter of speaking, a short time is better than no time at all. Most people don't feel that way because they want more in which is understandable. But sometimes it only takes just a short while to accomplish the needed task and to return back to our world. For example, Scotty. He knew that what he came to do was to send his family on a spiritual journey that they may not have ever taken hadn't he came and left when he did. He opened the door for his little sister and is bringing to his grandparents the learning they will need in order to help her.

Many times when there is a gifted child in the family, another has to pass on to open the family up to spiritual communication. It is never to be seen as fault or a reason for laying blame when this occurs. It is merely to be seen as one brave soldier giving his life or her life for another. It happens on a daily basis though most of the world does not yet have the eyes to see it.

In time, there will be notice of such noble intentions. But for now, it is hard. A baby that comes for only a brief time is a teacher of spirituality, a teacher who brings to the family a newfound faith in God. Because when the baby is brought back to God's world, they have to learn to trust that the baby is back in God's hands.

It is never meant to bring to the parents blame. Ever. There is nothing about blame that can bring healing. Healing comes from acceptance that there is a higher power at work and working to our benefit. Not our sorrow.

Babies are seen as angels when they return back to God's world. Whether they were lost as early as from conception to toddler, the meaning of their presence is to be a

125

messenger. Sometimes the smallest messages are the most powerful.

Chapter Fifteen

Learning How to Look at the Puzzle

Since the meeting in Thibodaux had appeared to comfort many families, Lisa and I began scheduling more of them. Once a month I returned to the town and gave a group reading. Judy always accompanied me. She told me she felt closer to Kyle by joining me, and I always appreciated her support. Each journey became a new experience and we went away with much more learning than we had ever expected. The children on the Other Side proved to be working overtime as they always brought comfort and healing for the grieving people who attended. But I found myself drained of energy for days after the meeting and didn't know how to replenish the supply. From my own experiences and understanding of the many books I have read on the subject, what I am doing when I read for some one is adjusting my vibration level to reach another realm. In doing so it takes a great deal of energy. I have found that for some reason, potatoes allow me to sustain the level for a longer length of time. However, readings still drain my body of energy once the meeting is over. I always asked Judy to stop at the nearest McDonald's for French fries after we left the angel shop. I craved them every time.

By the time we reached home, I was exhausted. It became a normal thing for me to just lie down for several days after I got back. I joked with my family that I barely had the energy left to stare, but it was exactly how I felt. I spent many Monday evenings after returning from Thibodaux just staring at the television, and it didn't matter whether it was on or off. I also noticed that many times the spirits accompanied Judy and me back home, and then I got messages all during the night while sleeping. I woke up even more tired the following day with my mind racing with information that I had to relay back to someone.

Since I didn't know how to limit the information I was receiving, I would sit at the meetings and relay the messages for however long it took. Sometimes I could end up giving one person twenty minutes of information and then move onto the next and do the same thing. When there were twelve people in the room that became a long and exhausting experience. While I was doing so, I had no concept of how it was draining me. Only when Lisa told me that we should take a break would I become aware of how tired I was.

During one meeting in late fall, Kyle saw an opportunity to teach me how to limit my information, and to move onto the next person. I had been giving each person a good deal of information and when I moved onto the next person, I gave her some messages that she acknowledged to be truth. Each time I told her something she nodded her head. But then I was shown a pot of chili. When I told her about it, she shook her head no.

"I see it very clearly," I said.

She shook her head no again.

So I paused a moment and waited for her to recall something significant that had happened to her concerning a pot of chili.

She shrugged and shook her head. "I haven't cooked chili or eaten it lately."

I sat there wondering what was going on. I could see a very big pot of chili and I couldn't move on until it was acknowledged. I had learned that sometimes it takes a little while for the event to surface. So I waited longer.

But she shook her head again. "No, sorry."

I shrugged next. I couldn't understand it. I didn't want her to make it fit. But there it was clearly an image in my mind. I glanced around at the others, all just as confused as I was.

Suddenly Judy spoke up looking a little embarrassed.

"Jim, my husband, just made a big pot of chili last night. I think Kyle is trying to acknowledge it."

130

Since no one else could make sense of it, I agreed that it must be Kyle. I tried to relay more information to Judy from Kyle but there was nothing but the pot of chili.

Judy and I looked at one another and shrugged. We didn't know why Kyle had done that.

When no more information came for the first lady from her child, I moved onto the next person. I gave the next person a significant amount of information from her child also, and suddenly I was shown the big pot of chili once more. I looked at Judy and said, "Kyle is doing it again. I see the big pot of chili."

Judy was as surprised as I was, then she said, 'Maybe that's your sign to move onto the next person."

I waited for more messages for the lady whom I had just read for, but there was nothing. So I knew Judy was right. Kyle's pot of chili was my indication to move on. He was showing me symbolically that I had given them the nourishment they needed and I needed to go onto the next person. It worked that day and when I left that evening, I wasn't quite as drained as I usually was.

Later, when some of the people complained of not being able to attend because of various reasons, I decided to do phone readings. The first time I held a reading over the phone, I worried that I would be all alone and more or less on my own with the information, but I should have known better and simply trusted. The children brought in whoever was scheduled to meet and the reading went well. Since I wasn't facing the clock at the time, I was giving a large amount of information, unaware of the time. Once again, I was shown a big pot of chili. I turned around to face my clock and it was exactly the time to end the reading. Kyle kept me on my toes again, reminding me how to stay on schedule.

I asked Kyle if the loss of time while giving readings is what it is like in the spiritual world. Here was his reply:

Exactly what it is like. Think now of a vacation time and when watches were not worn and everything was done as needed. That is what it is like here. If you were on a camping trip, you would eat when you felt hungry. You would sleep when you felt sleepy. You would find entertainment when you felt bored. You would enjoy the peace and quiet of existence.

The idea of time causes a stress factor in the physical life. Everyone believes they have to be somewhere doing something at an appointed time or they will miss their opportunity. Here we have no such boundaries or limitations. We are given opportunities but know that there are always more ahead.

That is why it is easier to heal the depressed souls who come to our side. They don't feel the pressure of having to exist in the lifestyle of the physical world. They are able to accept that everything happens in its appointed time.

When you listen to our world, you leave the physical world if only temporarily to experience the afterlife existence. That is why you lose track of time. Have you ever been so involved in a conversation with someone that time merely 'disappeared?' That is the same. You have left the physical body if only for a moment, to experience a higher learning that is shared with another.

Chapter Sixteen

Selecting a Piece That Doesn't Fit Yet

Months passed and I continued doing readings by phone and in Thibodaux. Heather and I learned to pay attention to the signs and notice when a new person had entered our home. Sometimes the symbology was as literal as the back door opening by itself. We would joke that someone new was visiting. Most times we were correct.

Christmas holidays were less eventful than we had expected but that was okay with us. The only thing out of the ordinary that occurred was our Christmas tree lights tended to have a mind of their own. The day we decorated the tree, we changed the star to an angel. Heather felt it seemed more appropriated, so we went along with it. Afterwards, the lights blinked at various times. Of course, Bob checked the fuses, changed the fuses, and rechecked the fuses, but it didn't matter. The children on the Other Side were letting us know they were around through the lighting, and we accepted it. Sometimes it became quite comical. There was no rhyme or reason as to why the lights would blink. On occasion they blinked while we were talking about one of the children on the Other Side. It would be a steady blinking while we talked. Other times it was just one blink when we made a significant statement.

One morning, I awakened Heather at 5:30 for school so that she would have extra time to study for a test. I went into the living room and plugged in the lights. The lights came on briefly then went out. I was so tired that morning that I sat on the loveseat in the dark, leaned my head against the pillow and accidentally fell asleep. At exactly six o'clock, the lights came back on brightly and woke me up, giving me the usual time to get ready before I had to take her to school.

Heather and I had gotten so accustomed to the lights blinking that after Christmas when we had to take our communicating tree down, we felt we had somehow lost connection with the children.

On January 19th, I woke up remembering a very vivid dream. I dreamed I had parked my red Grand Torino, the car I had when I was nineteen, at a hotel in Pensacola, Florida and decided to make my way back home on foot. I was carrying a pillow, my laptop, my purse, and a flashlight. I walked for miles and it was a beautiful countryside view, but it just did not seem like Florida. Later when it got dark, I realized that since I was barefooted, it could become dangerous. So I walked for a while longer. It got darker, and I noticed that there were no streetlights on the road I was traveling. It was hilly and curvy and I was beginning to get tired. My flashlight was growing dimmer, also.

I crossed the highway and went to a hotel that had mostly young people there. When I went in, I asked the older white-haired lady behind the counter if she had a phone book. I wanted to call a taxi to bring me back to my car because I could not walk any farther in the darkness. She handed me a phone book from the stacks she had behind her. After I took it, I sat down and began thumbing through the pages and a young, dark-haired guy came up and said he would take me back to my car. I told him it was many hours away, and it would take a good while to do so. He said he didn't care; he wanted to help me.

I looked at the old woman with a questioning eye, and she nodded that I should trust him. I gathered my things, and as we were going out the door, I said to her, "I don't even know his name." She answered, "You will get to know each other on the trip."

As we went outside, he led me to a Volkswagen. I asked him his name and he said Charles. I threw my things in the back seat and we left. Once we were on the road together, I woke up.

I knew the dream was a direct message dream. I felt it was more literal than symbolic but wasn't sure which part was which. Later that morning on the way to Heather's school, I told her about it in detail. I remember thinking that maybe someone name Charles had come to our home, and he was possibly around eighteen years old. In my dream I had the car that I owned when I was nineteen and had been dating a guy named Charles who was eighteen and who drove a Volkswagen.

As soon as I told Heather, the song "Sweet Dreams" began playing on the radio. We looked at each other and laughed. Then a Volkswagen cut in front of me on the boulevard and the next song that played was a song by Foreigner, popular when Charles and I had been dating.

So we gathered that yes, a Charles was visiting, possibly about eighteen years of age and he might be a foreigner.

A day later, Heather and I both began to notice how things concerning the West were being brought to our attention. First, I was sent a joke via e-mail about a cowboy. Then I was drawn to watching every western video we had. I kept expecting to hear the name Charles in each movie but I didn't. I was looking for some type of a connection. The pieces still weren't fitting.

Finally on January 23rd when I was least expecting it, I noticed a connection. Bob and I were watching *That 70's Show*. I'm a big fan of the 70's era and the show makes me laugh at the silliness of the "good ole days."

During the show, Bob commented, "Isn't the neighbor, Midge, being played by Tanya Roberts?"

I shrugged and said I didn't know who Tanya Roberts was.

"She was one of Charlie's Angels," he answered in a matter of fact manner.

"No, there are no Charlie's Angels on this show."

He nodded and said, "Yes. I know she was one of them."

It was during the commercial break that we were having this discussion and I remember thinking, "Who cares? Why are we arguing about something like this?"

When the show returned, Bob pointed her out and said, "I know that is Tanya Roberts."

I said, "Well, she wasn't on *Charlie's Angels*."

Bob, being a fan of their show in his younger years, gave me an acknowledging nod. "Oh, yes, she was. Just for a short time."

Heather walked in on what seemed like a serious debate and asked, "Who are you talking about?"

Bob pointed at Tanya Roberts and said, "She played on *Charlie's Angels*."

Heather looked at me, her eyes lighting up with familiarity. "Charlie?"

As soon as she gave me that look, I knew what was going on. Charles was trying to get my attention with the name Tanya Roberts.

Heather asked, "So what's that lady's name?"

I said, "Tanya Roberts."

She raised her eyebrows. "Wow, I've heard that name a lot lately."

"Really?" I asked, knowing we were onto something.

"Yes. On MTV, at school, lots of places," she answered.

"Why at school? I've never heard you mention a student with that name," I said.

"No, this was in the school newspaper. One of the faculty members had an article written in memory of her child. Her name is Tanya."

Bob just gave us his normal "oh they're at it again" look and went back to watching television.

In the meantime, Heather and I were quickly sorting more pieces of the puzzle. Who was Charlie and who was Tanya?

I asked Tanya why the children came to me in a dream with information that wasn't exactly accurate. Jason stepped in to reply:

The best way to describe it is through the game of Pictionary. Imagine playing that game with a person you have never met before as your partner. How would you get across messages to someone when you didn't know their dialect, slang or favorite television shows or music? You would start out with basic information. You would give universal thoughts as the clues. It wouldn't be as quick and accurate as two people who have known each other for years, but it would be a beginning.

What one person considers the best flavor of ice cream, another could detest. What one person calls a bay, another could call a sea. What one person calls a limo, another could call a Rolls Royce.

Symbolism is the universal language and that is why we use it to our advantage. But just like all languages, it can be misinterpreted.

Chapter Seventeen

Connecting Distant Pieces

Thursday morning, January 25th, while typing a message to a friend, I heard "Call Lisa." I didn't know why I was supposed to call her because I didn't have anything in particular to talk with her about at that time. But I kept hearing "Call Lisa."

Since I had learned not to disregard the unsolicited messages from the spirit world, I stopped typing and called her.

When Lisa answered the phone, she was surprised. She had a lady named Carol on the other line who had lost a daughter, Tanya, and at the very time my call beeped in, she was referring me to Carol for a reading.

I told her I would call her back later and that Jason and Tanya had obviously wanted to show their moms they were aware of what was transpiring.

Later, Lisa told me that Carol lived in Oregon and had somehow found Lisa's website by accident. They had begun writing to each other for about a week when Carol felt she should call Lisa. That was the same day that I called.

Since Carol was going to schedule a reading with me, I didn't want to know anything about Tanya. I had learned the less I know the more accurate the information becomes. I have always worried that if I am aware of the circumstances, my opinion or logical thinking may try to surface and cause me to guess instead of accurately read for the person. So the less I know about a situation, the better I feel going into it.

But this particular mother and daughter were an exception to my rule.

The next day, when my oldest son, Michael, was on his way to work, I was answering e-mail and didn't get up to tell him goodbye as I usually do. I had noticed he was running late, and I didn't want to delay him further so I let him go out the door without stopping him to chat.

Less than twenty minutes later, he called me from a pay phone. He had been in a head-on collision. I grabbed my purse and rushed out the door to be with him. All the while as I was driving, I kept saying, "I should have said goodbye. I should have stopped what I was doing and not cared if he were just a minute later. If I had stopped him, he wouldn't have been in that accident."

Suddenly, midway there, I acknowledged those thoughts and realized that was not my normal way of thinking. I am not one to say, "what if I had done it this way?" or "I should have done this" because I now believe there are no accidents. God has a plan for all of us. Each accident or coincidence after further study is discovered to be a part of the bigger picture of life. Like the puzzle, we only have scattered pieces that we try to make fit, yet we have no control over how or when they come into play.

My mother taught me that lesson well. When she was sick with cancer in 1995, she hid it from me. She had always been concerned with not burdening anyone with her problems. Though she was frightened, she kept her illness to herself for a very long time. When I learned about it a year later and much too late to be of help, I could not understand that if I were indeed so psychic, why couldn't I have sensed her illness somehow? How could I not have picked up that type of information from my own mother? But I learned that we are not shown everything. We are only shown what is needed or what we can handle at the time. I had always felt guilty that I should have psychically sensed she was sick and could have somehow prevented her death if I had known. I finally realized some things are just meant to happen, and we have no control over them whatsoever. Mama taught me to accept that and until the morning of Michael's accident, I thought I had.

After I reached the place where Michael had been in the accident, I saw his totaled Civic in the middle of the intersection and my heart sank. I couldn't imagine how he could have survived that. When I spotted him at the convenience store, I breathed a sigh of relief. For reasons unknown to us, the airbag did not inflate sparing him from the burns that can arise from such an impact. Though he was shaken up, he was physically unharmed. I thanked God and the children on the Other Side who had watched over him during the accident.

I also then realized that someone was trying to get my attention concerning those feelings I had experienced shortly before. Michael had been in two other accidents, and I hadn't thought that way when those had occurred. None of the accidents Michael had encountered were his fault. They were simply cases of being in the wrong place at the wrong time, which leads me to believe they were not accidents at all. Merely a rerouting of his path.

Later, while waiting in the doctor's office with Michael, I picked up a *Smithsonian Institute* magazine, not knowing exactly why. I scanned through the magazine and each time I stopped to glance down at a page, there was the name Charles on it. It happened three times. I began to wonder if the guy whom I had dated years ago had been killed in a car accident and he was coming through.

After a routine exam, the doctor told Michael he might have a little back and neck discomfort, but he could apply ice then heat to ease it. I remember teasing Michael and telling him I believed he had nine lives.

Once Michael and I were home and somewhat recovered from the ordeal of the morning, it dawned on me that Lisa hadn't told me how Tanya had died. Lisa said that Tanya had been added to her website and I wondered out of curiosity whether or not Tanya had been in a car accident.

I mentally spoke with Tanya and told her I wanted to check out the website to see if it were indeed an auto accident. I told her if she didn't want me to go any further to shut down my computer.

I turned on my computer, located Lisa's website and saw that yes, Tanya had been in an auto accident. I looked at her picture and said, "Okay, Tanya, if you don't want me to go any further, then shut down my computer."

Immediately, the screen went out, but not to screensaver, just to black. That was all I needed. I waited a few moments to see if it would come back on. It did and I got out of the website.

I realized that Tanya had joined our group of children and was trying to prepare me for the reading to come with her mother.

On January 29th, I had pretty much decided that Charles was the guy I knew back in the late '70s. I kept getting signs that pointed to him, but still there was the lingering doubt of why he was connecting with Tanya. Unless he had been in a car accident, also.

That morning, I was flipping through the channels and eating a Mexican TV dinner. I had begun to crave them and was eating them night and day. I assumed it was to help open my sinuses since I had caught a bad cold and was having difficulty breathing. I had learned in the past what to eat to help my body since taking medicine had become difficult to tolerate.

After much channel changing, I found an old episode of *Batman*. I love watching reruns of the show and the corny humor. It takes my mind off the seriousness and sadness of what I usually deal with on a day-to-day basis.

I got up to get a glass of water to cool down my burning mouth and when I returned, I noticed the episode of *Batman* was about Falseface. He was a villain who disguised himself as someone else. This episode was also staged in the old West. I sighed. I couldn't get a break!

When the second episode of *Batman* came on, I noticed that the Riddler was being played by John Astin instead of the regular actor who normally portrayed him. I knew then that Charles was not the Charles I thought he was. I was mistaking him for someone else. So the mystery continued.

By January 31st, I was really confused and didn't know how to put the puzzle together. That day I caught a quick portion of the episode of *The Brady Bunch* going to the Grand Canyon . . .also about the old West.

I had gathered that our new visitors were from the west after talking with Lisa and learning about Carol from Oregon. But why was I craving Mexican food daily and who was Charles?

On February 3rd, when Michael and Heather were going to the video store to pick up some movies, I felt the need to run outside and delay them. I told Bob I needed to stop them. I stalled and talked until they became annoyed. I kept feeling as if I had some control over their destiny by making them wait just a little longer. I was still shaken up about Michael's being in the previous accident and seeing the face of a girl on a website, made that possibility more real to me. Finally, Michael insisted on leaving before all the good movies were taken.

Suddenly, I felt a little silly and wondered again what had come over me. Then I recalled those feelings from the other day. I waved goodbye to them and came inside.

I sat down at my computer and wondered if it were Tanya trying to tell me something. When I logged in to my e-mail address, there was a message from Carol. She was asking to schedule a reading with me.

I wrote to her and explained the situation and that I truly believed Tanya was trying to make me understand that Carol felt she could have somehow prevented the accident, but it was not so. No one could have prevented it. Everything happened the way it was supposed to.

Carol wrote back and told me her husband told her he would have said no and three and a half hours later Tanya was in the accident. That had bothered her from time to time.

I told Carol that Tanya didn't want her mother to be concerned with his comment. It would not have changed things. She knows that better than we know it.

Tanya had made a direct attempt to put me into her mother's frame of mind so I would be better able to understand what she was going through. Guilt is a horrible thing to harbor, and she could not stand to watch her mother endure it any longer. She found a means of relaying that through me and it worked.

On February 4th, I realized I had been craving Mexican food for over a week and still hadn't figured out why. Later that day, a man called and left a message on my answering machine. He was speaking in a foreign language I couldn't understand. He left a very long message and then hung up. I tried the star 69 method to trace the call but it couldn't be traced. I assumed it was another message from the kids on the Other Side that I just couldn't figure out. Then ironically a song by Foreigner came on the radio, and I started laughing.

Not long after that, I walked into the living room and Rusty was watching an episode of *Gilligan*, which showed a scene with Ginger holding a séance and mentioning a whole fleet of ships coming in from Mexico. Again a Mexican clue that I couldn't make sense of.

Finally by February 9th, the day of the scheduled phone reading with Carol, the pieces began to interlock and slide into place.

Just before Carol was scheduled to call, I started coughing. I couldn't stop and thought I had better warn her that if during the reading I began coughing, I would have to stop the reading and reschedule it at another time. So when she called, I did just that, but amazingly enough, I didn't cough again until later that afternoon.

Tanya came through immediately and relayed information and images to me that Carol acknowledged, including the exact name of the cemetery where she was buried. She also described to me a music box that her mother had kept.

Being quite the skeptic that I am, I mentally asked Tanya to give my something a little more specific that couldn't be located through research or that Carol may have shared with

Lisa. I didn't want Carol thinking that Lisa had informed me about anything in any way. I hate relaying information that can be traced down in some way. I always wonder why bother with that? Anyone can do that. So Tanya complied with my request and showed me a bracelet. I relayed this to Carol.

"She's bringing me a bracelet," I began. "It is like diamonds but it is not real. It is something fake, but the bracelet is very important and sentimental to her."

There was a pause. I waited for Carol's acknowledgment, but there was only silence.

"She is showing me hugs and kisses symbols like it is something sentimental to her. But it is not real." I waited. Still no response. "She keeps bringing me this bracelet."

"Oh my God," Carol said. "My sister made a bracelet for Tanya with fake pearls and during the funeral I put the bracelet on Tanya because it was so special to her. Several people saw the casket close with her wearing the bracelet. But after Tanya's death, I was looking for a note Tanya had written to herself as a reminder about a friend's birthday. I had placed it in my jewelry box. At the time, I was on the phone with Tanya's friend when I opened my jewelry box, and there lying on top of the note was that bracelet. I couldn't understand how it got there when it had been buried with her . . .I had been questioning that."

I mentally thanked Tanya for coming through with something specific and then Tanya showed me the young man, Charles. So I asked Carol, "Did Tanya know a Charles shortly before she died?

There was a pause again.

"Charlie," she answered softly. "He is the one who was driving the car when she was killed."

"Is he on the Other Side with her, also?"

"Yes. He was killed, too."

"They are together and she shows me there is no blame. She doesn't want you to blame him. It was an accident." I remember the distinct feeling that Tanya was trying to get across. She did not want her mother to think harshly of this young man.

Later, I learned that Tanya loved Mexican food and was going to Taco Bell on the night of the accident. I also learned she had been speaking in French, a foreign language, the same day. The accident occurred on her ride home from Charlie's grandmother's house. I assumed that was who the white-haired woman was in my dream.

Tanya and Charlie were doing their best to play spiritual charades with Heather and me. We tried for several weeks to put together all the clues. By February 9th, the day of the reading, we could finally breathe a sigh of relief. Tanya and Charlie had gotten their messages through. It began with the dream of needing a ride home and a young man named Charlie offering me a ride. Then they became more specific when they got my attention with the reference to *Charlie's Angels* and Tanya Roberts. When that didn't work, Tanya encouraged a craving for Mexican food and made me catch the beginnings and endings of Foreigner songs. They did their very best to relay the messages. Understanding them was still somewhat new to me, but I was trying. They taught me that nothing is coincidental. Everything happens for a reason.

I asked Tanya why it is so important for the children to bring healing to their grieving parents. Here was her reply:

Have you ever stood behind a two-way mirror and been able to watch someone and know they couldn't see you? That is what it is like sometimes here. We see what our parents are going through and it is hard for us. We do everything we can to get their attention to let them know we are okay but sometimes our efforts are wasted. Sometimes the grieving parent just isn't ready to accept the loss. That is why when we appear at first with scents of our cologne or dreams or the feeling of our presence and when it isn't acknowledged, we back off for a little while and give the parent time to adjust to the circumstances. Then once we feel the parent is ready to accept where we are on a spiritual level, then we return even more powerful than before.

We communicate in ways that are the most accessible to us and also do not disturb the grieving parent's normal way of life. We are aware that they still must exist in the physical realm and deal with the realities that are present in their daily life. However we know that there are opportunities that we can jump on when presented that brings joy to the parent and so we do.

Some parents are more accepting earlier in the process so we give them information that seems to flood in. They become overjoyed yet confused as to whether or not they are 'truly' getting signs. That is when we search out mediums to confirm what they have suspected and bring it to light for them.

Other parents are not ready, so we come to them in dreams. God gave us the dreaming process for many reasons. We use it to relay messages to those who are not quite as open on a spiritual level. A dream in the physical world can be used as a scapegoat or a cover up for those who are worried

151

about their experience and how it affects the others in their life. However it still does the job that is needed.

In answer to your question, ask yourself this, if you were watching people suffer, wouldn't you try to do whatever it took to bring them comfort?

Chapter Eighteen

Adding Color to the Puzzle

On February 16th, I woke up from a strange dream. I had dreamed that I was walking down a long road with my friend, Pat, and we couldn't find the street that we were looking for. She kept telling me I needed to go one way, and I kept feeling I needed to go another way. We walked farther down the road and met up with some people who agreed with Pat and said the place we needed to go was two roads over. It didn't look like a road, but we would know it when we got to it. These people had a son named Joseph. They showed me a picture of him. They asked me if I could help their son and I said yes, that I would try.

We kept walking until we reached the street. It didn't connect to the main road, but it was a road up into the woods. We took the road and ended up at a school. I was barefooted and as we walked in, I noticed ants crawling all over the floor. I remember worrying that I was going to be bitten and since I am allergic to fire ants, I would swell up. I hurried out of there and after we began walking back, I woke up.

I lay there thinking about the dream, unsure of what it meant, but then I disregarded it and decided to say my usual protection prayer before climbing out of bed.

Since I am empathic, I have learned to protect myself before actually letting my feet hit the floor. I used to laugh or roll my eyes at people when they mentioned grounding themselves, but I have found that it makes a big difference in how I relate to the world once I began protecting myself. It has allowed me to discern what my emotions are and what I am picking up from others.

After saying the prayer, I then followed up with my usual prayer that I say for the children on the Other Side. Sometimes children whom I haven't thought about in a good while pop into my mind. Sometimes it is the regular ones. I always pray for Edgar and Kyle because I know without them I would never have begun this experience.

On that morning, when I said Kyle's name to myself, the alarm buzzer went off and scared me. It wasn't set to go off and shouldn't have. But there it was, buzzing away. I reached over and turned it off.

"What is it, Kyle?" I asked aloud. "What should I be alarmed about?"

There was no response.

A little while later as I was drinking my coffee and checking e-mail, I decided to write Judy and tell her what Kyle did. I told her that maybe we were going to have something "alarming" happen that day.

Later on that morning, around 10:00 while I was cleaning the house, I heard our doorbell ring. I was down the hall when it happened, and it surprised me because the doorbell was broken. It hadn't worked in months. Then in a few seconds, I heard someone pounding on the front door. I was expecting someone to deliver an office door that day, so I thought that's who it was, but suddenly on the way toward the front door, I got an image of the "alarm" that Kyle had scared me with that morning.

Since I was home alone, I waited for a moment debating whether I should answer it or not. The person pounded again. I couldn't understand why someone would pound on the door instead of just knocking. I went into the kitchen and peeped through the blinds onto the driveway to see if I could see the truck that was supposed to deliver the office door. Instead I saw a blue Mustang. I didn't recognize it, but I knew that whoever it was wasn't delivering the door.

I began wondering if it were possibly one of my oldest son's friends. It looked like a car for a young person. I began to feel foolish just standing there waiting and wondering and headed toward the door. Abruptly, the pounding began again very loudly and almost as if with frustration. I couldn't understand this behavior because all the doors were shut and locked, the blinds closed and no indication that someone was home.

I then went to my son's room, barely peeped out and through the blinds, saw a denim shirt but could not see a face. I waited a full ten minutes and when I went back to the kitchen the car was still sitting in my driveway. I thought that maybe the person was leaving a note for my son.

Finally fifteen minutes later, the car was gone, but not parked anywhere else in the neighborhood. This person had singled out my home to visit and I wasn't sure why. I figured it had to be a friend of my son's.

Two hours later, I went to see if there was a note on the door for my son. When I opened the door, a flyer fell down. It was trying to promote "alarm systems." I found that odd because our house already has an alarm and the faceplate should have been seen. Also, I wondered why this person didn't go to anyone else's home and why he pounded on my door for over fifteen minutes.

Kyle had seen that coming and pre-warned me with the alarm going off that morning. I found it very ironic that while I was saying a protection prayer for him, he was giving me an indication of how he was going to be protecting me. Only until much later did I learn this event had more meaning than I had been shown that day.

Saturday, while lying down to nap, I was just about to fall asleep, when I got an instant vision of the front grill of a car coming straight at me. I could see the Mustang symbol. It had such an impact that I startled and opened my eyes.

Three days later on February 19th, I was in Thibodaux and while speaking with Lisa, a lady came up and asked if I had done healing work before. I was totally caught off guard by the statement, because I hadn't shared that information with the people in that town.

Years before, I had learned through experience that I had also been blessed with spiritual healing abilities. I shared my gift with many, healing physical ailments that ranged anywhere from a headache to accepting a kidney transplant.

But I found the responsibilities that came with this gift too overwhelming for me at the time, so I refrained from using them.

Since I was surprised by her question, I didn't think before I replied and said, "Yes. Why?"

She said her son had been diagnosed with rheumatoid arthritis and she was wondering if I could say healing prayers for him.

Before I thought out my next response, I found myself asking, "What is his name?"

She said, "Joseph."

Suddenly the dream flashed into my mind. I remembered seeing the picture of Joseph and I just shook my head.

The lady questioned my response with a raised eyebrow.

"I'm sorry," I said. "It's just that I dreamed about him the other night. A child named Joseph, who would need my help."

She smiled, her eyes widening. "Really?"

"Yes. As a matter of fact, I sent an e-mail to my friend that morning telling her about the dream."

Then it dawned on me. I had also e-mailed Judy the same morning and told her about Kyle's setting off my alarm. Kyle had been trying to get my attention in many ways. First, he wanted me to pay attention to that dream and not be alarmed by what would happen concerning it. He knew that getting back into healing work was not my idea of fun. Then later that day, when he showed me the "alarm" image while someone was pounding on my door, he was trying to show me to trust him and that the children on the Other Side would indeed protect me even if it meant getting back to doing spiritual healing work.

I explained the dream and the situation concerning the alarm both to Lisa and the lady. I told them it had been a bit frightening waiting and wondering who was outside that door. Had it not been for Kyle's alarm, I might have opened it, thinking it was the man with the office door.

At that very moment, we saw the dark image of a man standing outside the door of the shop where we stood talking. We all looked at each other in surprise at the synchronicity of it. Someone began turning the knob trying to get inside.

Lisa went to the door, and it was her husband, Terry. "I don't believe this," she began. "If we wanted confirmation about what you just said, this is it! Terry used to drive a blue Mustang."

We all began laughing as Terry walked in oblivious to what had just transpired.

On the drive home that day, I began thinking about what had occurred and how the children were constantly teaching and preparing me for one thing or another. I began thinking about Joseph and whether or not I should go back into healing work again. Just as I thought that, a white bird swooped down in front of the van and flew off.

"I'll take that as a sign," I said.

Thirty minutes later while on the interstate, the alarm situation crossed my mind again and how the issues of trust and protection were being shown to me, wondering if that were a forewarning of what was to come. In that instant, I glanced in my rear view mirror and there was a white Mustang with the horse symbol on the grill. It seemed as if it had come up out of nowhere. I was driving 75 mph and it was right up on me. I got over to let it pass and noticed the license plate was from Arkansas . . .where Kyle went to college and played football.

I laughed and said, "Okay, Kyle, I get it now!"

I didn't question the healing issue again, but I learned much later that the blue Mustang meant something else altogether!

I asked Jason if it is all harps and halos where he is. Here was his reply:

Life on this side is very much the same as life on your side. Only we are so capable here of understanding our emotions, our fears, our experiences. The physical body places a harsh demand on the soul for it must endure the aches and pains of reality. Over here we are not concerned with that so we are able to live life more fully. We are able to do our learning in which involves forgiveness of others and of ourselves for not being the perfect person we had sometimes hoped to be. We are allowed to experience and see what it is like from this side as we watch your side make the mistakes that we have made. It is like watching little children begin to ride a bike and fall down only to get back up again. Some get up and try again. Some just keep falling and some ride away smoothly with their newly found knowledge.

We are not limited in our learning here for our teachers are coming from many lifetimes of wisdom. We have our own guides who teach us what we have not fully learned in the physical journey. We are taken to masters of science, biology and history to learn what we need to accomplish. There is much to take in over here.

Whether or not it is all halos and harps depends on your view of the beauty that we encounter. We are able to view the landscape, if you will, at what we find to be most enjoyable. Just as you are able to hit the button on a remote control and see different scenery on your television set, we are able to blink and be where we need to be. For time is not an essence of what we do. Time is man made. Here we exist in the moment of where we need to be, when we need to be.

Think of your world for a moment. Then envision it to be everything you would like it to be. It is more than that.

Chapter Nineteen

Filling in the Empty Spaces

One morning in the spring, I was cleaning out old papers in my computer room and trying to rearrange things when I heard, "check your mail." I stopped what I was doing and logged in. There was a message from Gloria, Emily's mother. She had decided she wanted to meet with me.

The arrangements were finally made and Heather and I met with Gloria and her two other grown daughters. We met at a library midway between our two hometowns.

We were able to find a room in the back and visit for a short while. It was an awkward situation for all of us at first, but then Emily came through and gave me information that eased the tension. I asked Gloria if Emily had a cat that nipped at her ankles.

Gloria gave me a strange look, smiled and nodded. "Yes, the cat was known to do that, why?"

I said, "Because this morning before leaving, I kept getting the feeling that I was being bitten by a cat while reading my e-mail and Emily showed me it was her cat."

Gloria's eyes began to tear up. "That cat was hit by a car this week and we had to have it put to sleep. I knew Emily would be upset."

I shook my head slowly. "No. Don't you see? She's not upset. The cat is with her now. That was how she was able to show you that."

Gloria's expression changed. "Really?"

"Oh, yes. The pets cross over, also. I see them all the time."

Gloria took a deep breath and sighed.

I could tell she was extremely nervous. I felt sorry for her and kept mentally asking Emily what she wanted me to tell her mother next. Emily kept telling me to wait.

Finally, I asked, "Did Emily have mood swings?"

Gloria shot a glance toward her oldest daughter and they both broke into laughter.

"That's putting it mildly," the daughter said.

Heather started smiling. "Well, that explains that."

Gloria gave Heather a questioning look.

"We pick up what the spirits in our house are feeling and Mom and I have been so moody lately we didn't know what was going on." Heather then looked at the sisters. "Did Emily like to eat a lot?"

One sister raised her eyebrows and said, "Yes. All the time. She was a very big eater for as little as she was."

Heather said a soft, "Yes!"

"Heather and I have been eating like crazy for the past few weeks and didn't know why," I explained to Gloria.

Gloria seemed to relax finally, and I could feel the awkwardness slipping away.

"Are you ready for some messages from Emily?"

Gloria tensed up a bit again, then exhaled. "Okay, go ahead." She said it as if I were going to give her horrible news.

"Don't worry," I assured her. "Emily is only going to tell you what you are ready to hear. She didn't bring us this far to scare you off."

Gloria gave me a half smile and nodded.

I then relayed messages to her that made her think, smile and nod to her daughters.

They would agree or disagree about the simple information that I began to relate.

Finally, I ended the messages with one last bit of information. "Emily wants me to tell you that she knows you broke the antique doll that you gave her. It was an accident. And she knows it."

Gloria started crying. Heather handed her a tissue from her purse.

After she had regained her composure, she spoke. "Before we arrived today, I mentally asked Emily to tell me something through you that only I knew. That no one else could possibly know, and then I would believe that she was okay . . .and no one knew I broke that doll. No one."

All eyes were watering by then, and I knew that Emily had succeeded in what she wanted to accomplish.

Heather and I drove home that day feeling as if it had all been worth it. During the ride back, she told me something I had never considered. She told me Gloria had confided in her later that she thought I would tell her something concerning how Emily died, and she was so frightened of getting a picture in her mind that she wouldn't be able to erase. It had been the major holdup concerning meeting with me. I was so thankful to Emily for not frightening her mother, and I learned that what I had suspected all along was true. The children on the Other Side that come to me are not interested in catching the criminal. They are interested in helping their grieving parents heal.

I asked Edgar how could mothers be better able to accept the murder of their child. Here was his reply:

It takes a much higher level of acceptance to be able to accept the murder of one's child. The acceptance has to come from the heart, the place of knowing that the God force is with their child.

I will give you reference to a physical example. Suppose a mother had two children. One child was extremely intelligent, excelling in all that she tried. Suppose the other child was severely handicapped and unable to do quite as much, even simple things like pickup after himself. If the handicapped child were to destroy a precious antique or family heirloom, it would be forgiven because the cause is of a different form. However if the prodigy child did so, it would be a cause of great distress, unforgivable and infuriating to the parent to witness such an event.

On a higher level, on which the murdered children have reached, they see their murderer as the handicapped child, the one who needs forgiving because his connection to the higher sources aren't intact.

This is how a parent can reach that point of healing and forgiveness when their child has been murdered. They find in them the part of them that realizes that something is askew in the physical being of the murderer.

Acceptance that all is in the force of the energy realm brings about the harmony that is needed when the heart feels ravaged.

Chapter Twenty

Looking at the Puzzle From a Different Angle

A short time later, when I was asked to help with an investigation concerning a missing person, I learned that the children on the Other Side were also preparing me to help the children on this side. I wasn't very excited about helping to locate a missing person because I do not feel that I am very good at solving crimes nor do I like putting myself in that position. When working with the police department I am not told anything, nor am I given any acknowledgment of whether or not my information is correct. I merely tell them what I am shown and that is that. I never find out if I have been of help or not because the detectives are not allowed to discuss anything that isn't already public knowledge. I find it to be difficult work at times. It is very much a negative activity. When I work with the spiritual side of crimes, I am taken into a place that can be frightening and sometimes unsettling. The images I receive can make me shiver. I have empathically experienced murder victims' state of emotion during the time of death, and it isn't a place I like to visit for long.

But this mother pleaded with me, so I agreed. Paula's husband had been missing and presumed dead with no evidence of who or why. She confided in me that it had been two years, and she no longer knew how to comfort her daughter. She didn't want to scare her, but she also didn't know what to tell her.

Whenever I am asked to work on a case, I find myself playing detective and suspecting everyone. Since I am not given any more information than the public receives, I am left to speculate for myself, which means that I always suspect the person who asks for help. I guess I have watched too many detective shows and tend to look at the obvious suspect last and the least obvious first. So I found myself wondering if Paula had murdered her husband and disposed of him. But then why would she seek me out? It didn't make sense, and yet, I still toyed with the idea that it was possible.

In the beginning, Paula gave me the location of where her husband was last seen. I drove there one day and spent some time. I kept having the nagging feeling that I shouldn't be there, that I was getting into something that could be dangerous. The first image that popped into my head was a blue Mustang. I wondered if her husband had driven that type of car. Then, I assumed whoever had done this could possibly have driven a Mustang. I also acknowledged that it could have been the last person driving in that area who had nothing whatsoever to do with the crime. As I said, I don't claim to be good at doing detective work. I agreed to help because I felt it was part of my purpose, that maybe I could bring some answers to Paula and her daughter that would comfort them.

I sat there a moment longer, closed my eyes and relaxed, trying to pick up something that might have been of help to someone. Nothing.

During the long drive home, I wondered why I had agreed to help her. What was the purpose when I knew that I was probably only going to get her hopes up for nothing? Or what if I did give her accurate information and if she were guilty, would she worry that I suspected her? At that moment, a blue Mustang flew past me on the highway. Did the murderer drive a blue Mustang? There was no response from any of the children. Nothing.

I got home and noticed the television was on and no one was watching it. Everyone had gone to their bedrooms and left it playing. There was a show on that was making fun of the movie *The Sixth Sense*. I sat down and rested a bit from the drive. I was tired and not sure what I was supposed to do next when I noticed a magazine on the floor that was opened to a page, advertising the television show *Andy Griffith*.

I laughed at the way the kids were trying to get my attention by combining the show and the movie to mean psychic police work, but thought no more of it.

A few days later I caught an actual episode of *Andy Griffith* and the story was about Opie's doing something secretive to help a needy child, when all along Andy had assumed that Opie was being selfish and spending money on himself. That episode kept haunting me and I couldn't understand why. What was it about this particular show that was trying to get my attention?

For a week, I noticed the blue Mustangs everywhere. There was even one on a commercial for sale at a used car lot. I only seemed to notice them when I was thinking about the situation with Paula. I was so sure that the crime involved a blue Mustang. Why else would I keep seeing them?

By the weekend, I had almost given up trying to understand what I was supposed to be connecting with since I had been shown so little. Then, out of the blue, Heather brought up the time that my father had walked out of her closet and scared her.

Finally it dawned on me! Was Paula's daughter getting information from her deceased father but Paula believed she was making it up? Was that the kids' intentions when I received the simultaneous clues about Andy's not believing Opie and the movie *The Sixth Sense*?

I decided that it was, and I scheduled a meeting with Paula the next week.

We sat facing each other in the café, and I waited until the right time to confront her with my concerns.

"Paula, how do you think that I receive information concerning murders or missing people?"

She shrugged. "I haven't ever really thought about it in great depth." She sipped her coffee and thought a moment. "I guess I figured that you sensed it some way."

"Have you ever seen the movie, *The Sixth Sense*?" I asked.

171

She gave me a questioning look. "Yes. What about it?"

"What did you think of it? Do you believe that children see dead people?"

She laughed. "Oh, I don't know. I believe they think they see them." She hesitated then frowned. "You know, in the beginning, Angela told me that she saw Roger, but her therapist told us that it was just part of the grieving process. You know, they miss the parent so much that their imagination creates a comfort zone for them to slip into."

I looked at Paula in disbelief. Then I was quickly shown an image of my own childhood. When I was younger, I had many psychic abilities that scared my mother. I remember very clearly at four years of age telling her about a vivid dream, and then it occurred just as I had told it. It scared her so much that she told me about the superstition that it was bad luck to tell dreams before breakfast because they would come true. I was well into my thirties before I realized why she had told me this. She knew if I waited until after breakfast and went out to play, I would forget my dreams and she wouldn't have to hear them. It was very scary for a mother back in the early '60s to accept that her four-year-old daughter could predict the future.

I realized at that moment it is just as scary now for some mothers to accept that their children can see deceased loved ones.

"I don't believe that Angela is making it up," I told her.

Paula gave me a wry grin. "So I'm supposed to believe her?"

"Well, let me ask you this. Has she been known to make up outlandish stories to get attention?"

Paula's face grew serious then she slowly shook her head no.

"Would you consider her to be a fibber?" I continued.

Again, Paula shook her head no.

"Does she seem reluctant to tell you about this?"

Paula nodded slowly, seeming to make sense of what I was getting at.

"Speaking from my own experiences, when a child is very hesitant in discussing what they see, it is because they are just as frightened by it as we are and they're looking for comfort from a parent to tell them that they aren't crazy." I waited for Paula to digest what I had told her before I went on.

"You see, children are more apt to see the deceased parent than the grownups in the family. The reason is because they have not been told they can't." I paused a moment. "As adults we have taught ourselves not to believe in the supernatural because it is safer and less scary. The movies and television portray those experiences as frightening and gory, and so we don't want to be a part of that world." I watched the look of enlightenment spread across her face. "But Paula, it's not like that for me. I don't normally see gory and frightening stuff. The spirits present themselves to me in an acceptable manner." I smiled at her. "Otherwise I won't help them."

Paula took a deep breath and sighed. "Do you mean I should believe that Angela has seen her father?"

"Why would you not?"

"Well, it would mean that he is dead."

I spoke my next words carefully, not wanting to cause her further grief. "And maybe that's what he's trying to get across to you. Lay this to rest. Listen to your daughter. Let her tell you what she has seen and heard. If Roger is on the Other Side, it must be very important for him to get you to open up to this way of thought. For Angela's sake."

Paula's eyes watered with tears as she nodded slowly. "I'll talk to her tonight."

A week later I spoke with Paula by phone. Her voice was different. She just had to share her news.

"You should have seen the look of relief on Angela's face when I told her it was okay to see her father," Paula began. "She started crying and thanked me so many times for not thinking she was crazy."

"What did you tell her?" I asked.

"I told her that I wanted her to share whatever she saw or heard about her father and not to be worried about what I would think." Paula drew in a breath. "You know, I can't believe what a difference it has made in her attitude. She was so withdrawn before. But now she's starting to open up to me like you wouldn't believe."

I laughed. "Oh, believe me, I understand. But just a word of advice . . .don't probe her for information. Ever."

Paula became silent for a moment then asked, "Why not?"

"Because if Angela feels pressured to get answers and see her father, it will all shut down."

"What do you mean?"

I could hear the frustration in Paula's voice. "When Roger comes to her, it is to comfort her. She is not a medium with whom you can ask questions and receive answers. If she feels as if you are pressuring her, I can guarantee you that she'll stop seeing him because he'll stop coming to her."

"I don't understand," Paula replied.

"Why do you think you were led to me in the first place after all this time?"

"I was running out of answers."

"Roger led you to me. He knew that Angela was aware of his presence and that she was having a difficult time telling you about it. She was suffering an inner turmoil as most children do who have visits from loved ones and are unable to share it with others."

"So, do I just drop the search?"

"That is your call. My job is to help heal the families, not solve the crimes."

Paula sighed heavily.

"Be there for Angela and listen to her stories. No matter how farfetched they may seem at the time, don't make an ordeal out of it. Just acknowledge her experiences and allow her to find peace with it. In the long run, you will see what a healing experience it will be for both of you."

After we hung up, I noticed a blue Mustang passed by. Then it all made sense. The first time I was instructed to pay attention to a blue Mustang was when Kyle buzzed my alarm clock. He showed me that the children would protect me with their guidance as long as I followed it. The next week, the blue Mustang came into play concerning my reentering the world of spiritual healing work. Again, the children were showing me to trust and know that I would be protected.

Later, when I was asked to participate in an investigation that I was leery of, the children showed me many blue Mustangs to remind me not to be alarmed but to trust them. I was not to fear for my safety but to know that the circumstances brought to me were not to solve the crime, but to bring a healing experience to Paula's family. A different kind of spiritual healing.

I asked Edgar why children are open to the Other Side more so than adults. Here was his reply:

A child coming into this world appears to be a newborn. Let's look at it in a different manner. Suppose you had been living in Germany for the last four years. You learned about their lifestyle, their pleasures, and their method of communication. Once you returned to your home, you would not have immediately forgotten them, would you? Of course not. They stay with you for a long time. Until you reacquaint yourself with your home lifestyle once again and then the lifestyle of Germany begins to fade. You no longer have the need to communicate in that form.

It is the same with a newborn coming to your world. They have been in the hands of God until it was time for them to make their appearance. They have been in the spiritual realm for quite some time so they have learned the method of communication that is needed to 'see and hear' the others in the spiritual world.

As the child grows and becomes more accustomed to the physical world, the past ways of communication fade and the current activities take hold. Only unless a parent nurtures and allows the child to communicate with the spirit world will there be continuity. Just as if you stopped speaking the German language you learned because there was no longer a need for it. However if you continued to speak it, it would not leave you.

The children never lose what they have learned in the spiritual existence, they merely readjust to what is needed in the physical.

Chapter Twenty-one

Putting in the Last Pieces

On March 22nd, almost two years since Edgar had first come to my home, I was standing in the printing shop examining my new business cards. They were just right. Everything on them turned out the way the children on the Other Side had planned. I thanked the people who had so kindly allowed me to start over and redo the design so many times, before going to my van.

When I turned on the radio, the song "I Could Not Ask For More" by Edwin McCain was playing. It was exactly how I felt.

The following night, Judy, Pat, and I were scheduled to go to a new group meeting for mothers who had lost children held near Lafayette. The week before, when I had been going through the card ordeal, I had craved spaghetti all week. Not only was I craving it, but I had also heard many different people tell me they were eating it that week. The word "spaghetti" kept coming up in my conversations. I had no idea why until that morning, while saying my protection prayer. The young man's name whose mother I did a reading for the year before came to mind. He had told me during the reading that she had cooked spaghetti. So when his name came into my protection prayer unexpectedly, it dawned on me that he was the one trying to get my attention. It had been exactly a year since I had read for his mother, and he was returning for reasons I hadn't foreseen.

Just as I was backing out the driveway on my way to pick up Pat, Heather came running out the door and handed me an angel ornament. She said, "Give this to one of the ladies. You will know who."

That night, during the meeting, it came together. The very first lady whom I read for had lost a daughter named Allison. The young man who had brought me the craving

179

for spaghetti had also said Allison's name during the reading exactly a year before. I knew she was the lady who was supposed to get the ornament. At the end of the reading, I handed it to her and told her what Heather had said. She told me she collected angel ornaments just like the one I gave her. Allison led Heather to do that. Of that, we are sure.

Since the young man mentioned Allison's name a whole year before, it was a confirmation for me that the children on the Other Side had been planning my future for a very long time.

The meeting lasted until very late that night and it was after midnight when the children on the Other Side reminded me of their continuous protection.

I had already picked up my van at Judy's house and then dropped off Pat, when I reached the highway leading to my subdivision. I was extremely tired. I could barely keep my eyes open, so I jokingly asked Kyle to make sure they played an upbeat song to keep me awake. When I turned on the radio, I heard "Paradise City" by Guns and Roses. That kept me awake. Riding down the highway, I came to the traffic light leading into my subdivision. I needed to turn left but my light was red. I waited for what seemed like a long time because I was so tired. Finally when the green arrow appeared, I was getting ready to floor it as I usually do when I heard very loudly and clearly, "Don't go!" I hesitated a moment and just as I was about to hit the accelerator, I heard "DON'T GO!" So I paused. Before I could even consider it again, a car in the oncoming lane flew through the red light right in front of me. If I had not taken their advice, I would have been hit.

I drew in a deep breath and sighed with relief, then thanked the children for their protection.

In the months to follow, through research with books and interviews with people who know symbology, I learned why the children chose the symbols they did.

Kyle brought to me the squirrel, the black crow and the starfish. Squirrels are symbolic of being prepared for what is to come just as they store up food for the winter. Kyle was

180

preparing me for the different situations that I would encounter. The black crow is symbolic of the mystical events that happen in our lives all the time. He brought the crows as a reminder for me to always pay attention to the signs. Since the starfish is a creature that has no eyes or ears and bases its survival upon its sense of touch, Kyle brought this symbol to remind me always to trust my instincts.

Jason brought to me butterflies to remind me to make the necessary changes when the opportunities present themselves. Since I am one who doesn't handle change very well, the butterfly appears on occasion to remind me that change doesn't have to be traumatic, but can promise something even better.

Edgar chose spiders in the beginning because they have been regarded throughout history as the guardian of ancient languages and alphabets and as teachers of writing. He knew I was destined to write this book to bring comfort to grieving families. He wove the web one strand at a time, teaching me new languages and ways to communicate with the spirit world with each new child he brought to my home.

Why did Edgar make sure that I heard songs by the Doors? When I first began writing this book, I had no clue, but I knew I would be led to the answer to that question by the time I had completed it. Several weeks ago, I watched the movie, *The Doors,* one more time and Edgar gave me the answer.

In the movie, Val Kilmer, who plays the part of Jim Morrison, says one line that got louder on my television as I watched it.

The line is a quote from the poet, William Blake, whose writing was inspired by mystical visions: "When the doors of perception are cleansed, things will appear as they truly are. Infinite."

I knew Edgar was talking to me the moment I heard those words and will remember that line the rest of my life. For in those words I have learned that our spirits truly do live on forever.

Afterword

When I first began writing this book, it was to help parents who have lost children be able to better accept their loss with more peace in their hearts that their children are okay. That has been a commonly asked question: Yes, I know they are on the Other Side, but are they okay?

Since I have completed this book and still have children come to my home quite frequently, I have learned the children are more okay than we think. I have also learned the child is just as concerned about the parent as the parent is about the child.

The love that a parent and child share is an energy form that does not disappear with death. It remains throughout eternity.

It has been three years since Edgar appeared in my home on that chilly November night. He, along with the other children, have taught me much in that length of time but the most important lessons were that of faith and trust. Just because we cannot see something does not mean it isn't there. When it is time to see it, we will.

Throughout the summer and into the fall, Kyle, Edgar, Tanya, Emily, Jason and Russ have brought new children to my home in hopes of reuniting them with their parents. They forewarned me about the September 11th suicide bombings, and even prevented me from flying out on November 16th when the Atlanta airport was delayed for four hours. Waiting outside with 10,000 people who were tense and fearful for that length of time would have been an empath's worst nightmare. But, because of the kids' guidance and my faith in them, I cancelled my flight to Orlando at 5:30 that morning, and did not have to suffer through the extended layover in Atlanta. I drove to Orlando instead, and reached my grandmother's house sooner than I would have if I had flown and it was a much more enjoyable trip.

The children on the Other Side continue to guide me and teach me one lesson after another. Sometimes the lessons are harsh. Sometimes they are gentle. It all depends on what I am ready to handle at the time. Just as the children come to the parent when they are ready and no sooner.

My goal in this lifetime is to reunite as many children on the Other Side with their parents that I can. And as my good friend, Judy Collier has said, "If you can help just one person, then it is worth it."

Note to the Reader

For those interested in contacting Linda Hullinger for a phone reading or group reading, please write to her at:

P.O. Box 82482
Baton Rouge, LA 70884
e-mail: puzzlewithoutabox@yahoo.com
www.lindahullinger.com

Referrals

Judy Collier
Quit Kissing My Ashes, 2002
1-800-479-9230
www.quitkissingmyashes.com

Lisa Guidroz
Grief Recovery Consultant
P.O. Box 453
Schriever, LA 70395
E-mail: BrysonsAngels@webtv.net
www.brysonsangels.bizland.com

William Closes the Box

During the writing of this book, a guide, William, who has been with me since I first began the class on spirituality, has led me to different arenas of thought about how to approach the religious aspect of my work. Being raised Baptist and then converting to Catholic in my early thirties, I have experienced two different types of teachings. Since William is on the Other Side, I felt he could help answer my question that could apply to any religious belief. I asked him how could I explain that God directs my work. Here is what he said:

In trying to find suitable explanations one must first understand the concept of what is. And by that it is meant to understand the concept of a loving God who cares not whether or not you have expressed your beliefs in him. He knows what you believe, regardless of what you portray to others or feel that you know about yourself. It is of that, that I bring to you a simple statement. In God, everything is possible. God creates the energy that you use to communicate with the children. When your communications heal someone, and bring about a restored faith in life itself, how can it come from anyone but God?

Compare suffering to comforting. Which would God choose to bring about to the people who are grieving? It matters not whether they believe in the Catholic religion or the Baptist. Both religions teach the same thing: a respect for God and all in the universe.

Why is it difficult for others to accept what you do? It is just as the world was not ready for the disciples and their teachings. In time, it will be easier to accept and

187

understand. How long did it take for the world to realize that the earth was not flat? Fear of shattering the belief system prevents many from stepping out and learning more. Everyone needs something to hold on to when someone so dear to us has been taken away, and the belief system is what gets one through it.

Everyone will see in time that we are all of one God, a loving and compassionate God, who will do what is needed to comfort those in grief.